The Clockwork Courtesan

Timothy Black

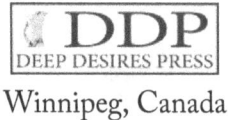
DEEP DESIRES PRESS

Winnipeg, Canada

Developmental editor: Craig Gibb
Proofreader: Francisco Feliciano

Published June 2022 by Deep Desires Press, an imprint of Story Perfect Inc.

Deep Desires Press
PO Box 51053 Tyndall Park
Winnipeg, Manitoba R2X 3B0
Canada

Visit http://www.deepdesirespress.com for more scorching hot erotica and erotic romance.

The Clockwork Courtesan

Chapter 1

Charlotte Frost snorted in derision at the seven-foot-tall automaton holding his raging hard-on on the deck of her airship.

"Put it away, Doll. I'm not here to fill up on empty calories."

Tiny brass mechanisms in the Doll's facial shell manipulated the pliant ivory of its smooth features into the expression of a hurt puppy who doesn't understand why its owner is being so cruel. The process, while amazing in its own way, did nothing to add to his sexual allure.

"But you are here to refuel, mistress," the Doll protested, methodically stroking his pristine pale cock to keep it erect. Gusting winds blew up from the Mediterranean Sea below, its glittering surface a half-mile down from where the *Harlot's Promise* had docked with the floating city of Godmother. Charlotte briefly entertained the thought of throwing the Doll overboard instead of sending it down the boarding ramp back into the city before dismissing the idea as churlish.

The machine's jerking motion on its phallus made it

glint in the afternoon light, as if he was desperately trying to catch a firefly dancing along his dick. While the mechanical men were never "not in the mood," when their activation chakra wasn't being stimulated the automatons were forced to resort to more old-fashioned techniques. Replicating human emotions and sexual desires in Doll form unfortunately carried over such minor imperfections in the process. But she didn't need her tantric engineering abilities to bring the Doll to arousal; Charlotte was five feet and change, with raven-black hair that tumbled down her back when not drawn into a working ponytail, eyes blue and sharp like chipped ice that sparkled as bright as the small ruby on her forehead, and tawny brown skin that took on a gold sheen under the fading sun. Curvy with ample hips and bosom, Captain Frost's comely shape hid muscles earned through a lifetime of the duties on sky ships. Even though she wasn't quite as well-endowed as some of the other tantric aviatrixes, she'd sent more than a few men scurrying to hide their arousal without even touching their auras. And that was without considering the dark scarlet flight leathers she was wearing that pulled tight in all the best places, complete with a matching herring-bone bustier.

Charlotte had to admit the Doll was physically impressive as well. Perfectly hairless, he was a literal sex machine, with sculpted ivory plates in the same location as muscles, connected by a series of brass gears and hydraulics covered by a translucent "skin" formed from the mystic energies powering him. The perfect abs and buttocks naturally drew the eye around the cut V of his loins to his most augmented feature. The ivory muscle-plates were softened by the magical energy running through his frame into a warm approximation of flesh while a transparent sheen of silken skin connected the muscle plates into a seamless whole. The brass orbs of his eyes might even be called lovely, if there'd been any spark of intelligence in them.

He was little more than a mindless mechanical though, a statue come to life whose defining feature was a member that could fill the most demanding of lovers to satisfaction over any amount of time. His cock was twelve inches at least, with a thickness that would put a natural man to shame. This Doll was one of Erin's creations, without a doubt. She had no sense of style or subtlety. Jackhammers were her idea of foreplay, as Charlotte had found out the one time she'd been drunk enough to spend an unsatisfying night with the captain of the guard...and Lauren...

Hot anger rose up in Charlotte's chest, the Doll an insult to her. Charlotte caught herself before her fist flew out; it wasn't the machine's fault. But that didn't mean the aviatrix had to tolerate the Doll's presence on her ship.

The oblivious mechanical protested as the aviatrix pushed him down the Liberty Ship's boarding plank in the warm summer air back toward the city, never altering his rhythmic masturbation. Although the airship was held in firmly in place with the docking clamp a few feet below, the sturdy boarding ramp was the only safe way to traverse the twenty feet of open air between the ship and the flying city without balancing on the clamp itself, which was only inches in width. Sunlight played across the cresting waves a half mile below in a disorienting pattern that made

Charlotte glad of the guardrails on the ramp. Although the aviatrix had no fear of heights, she was still keenly aware of each creak from the boarding ramp as they clomped down it to the steel hatchway that led into the floating city.

Godmother was a majestic metropolis in the clouds. Built to be a bastion from the world, the giant city was at its core a fortress for the battered and the abused. Her hull and superstructure were entirely composed of rudimentary libidium, runed and bolted with care. By infusing ground crystal and magic into the smelting process the first Matriarchs discovered the alloy, using only the materials they had on hand. As strong as steel at a tenth the weight, the metal's true supernatural abilities manifested when charged with tantric energy, reversing the laws of gravity and allowing for the creation of both the city and her airships. Streaked through with whorls and differing shades, libidium had an appearance like Damascus steel save for one key difference: the magic had tinted the markings as various shades of purple. Constructed in secret by the first generation of tantric engineers, the materials for Godmother were drawn from pots, pans, old tools and other scraps of iron and steel surreptitiously donated and stolen. To compensate for the crudity of the available materials massive amounts of magic had been infused into Godmother's libidium. The pig iron origins and copious mystical additive had led to a darker tint with far more violet running through it than normal and earning her the moniker of Amethyst City.

Largely freed from the structural limitations of steel, the Matriarchs had built a series of curving towers that wove in and out of each other in a dazzling organic pattern that looked as if a bouquet of gigantic sweet pea blossoms rested within the loving embrace of a water lily's petals. The petal-walls were inscribed with the silver runes that helped generate the flight aura that supported Godmother's massive weight. The multiple sails ringing the city that helped to steer her ponderous bulk were as a lily pad, carrying the most dangerous and titanic flower the world had ever seen. Tantric engineers refused to sacrifice form for function, and through their efforts had married both into a practical art that accomplished feats normal machinists could only dream of.

In contrast, the Liberty Ships were originally adapted from sea-faring vessels and still owed much of their structure to their predecessors, but with a graceful beauty that defied normal structural constraints. There were few moored at the docks that interspersed the city's steering sails, as most captains valued their freedom far more than the average Godmother inhabitant. Liberty Ships generally had a top deck, a quarterdeck, and then the engineering deck, all contained by a wooden hull that elegantly swept from a large rear forward to a narrower keel in a teardrop shape. A network of libidium rebar snaked through the support beams within, lending both structural integrity as well as flight when charged. Two large pontoon engines powered by the ship's crystal core were mounted port and starboard, each having a massive propeller that served as the thrust to the libidium's lift. When combined with the pair of triangular sails that could be unfurled from collapsible curved masts that extended skyward and seaward from the stern like a courtesan's fan, it gave Liberty Ships unmatched maneuverability. The colorful paints that captains favored on the hulls of their airships made the fleet look like a school of supernatural tropical fish of monstrous proportions; the *Harlot's Promise* itself was a vibrant shade of red that matched Charlotte's control ruby.

Liberty Ships were the material embodiment of what the first tantric engineers, of what any oppressed minority, desired most: freedom. Not just for oneself, but for all others who have tasted the lash and the boot. Crewed by aviatrixes who felt the impetus to help the grounders, Liberty Ships were infamous for spiriting away the lewd, the lascivious, and the improper to the safety of more welcoming climes. Husbands both rich and poor had awoken from drunken rampages only to discover their beleaguered families had escaped into the night, to lives free of abuse. Although precious few of the rescued chose a life among the clouds with the aviatrixes, by putting hundreds of miles between the victims and their tormentors scattered Matriarchy safehouses provided something many abused had given up on altogether: hope.

Lauren and Erin had stolen that hope for the future from Charlotte, and the insultingly crude Doll they'd sent to her was proof positive that they did not truly comprehend the pain they'd inflicted.

Although the automaton was beautiful in the same fashion of all his kind, perfectly willing to go down on her until she couldn't see straight, slam into her for days on end, or endure any torture she could come up with, it was all a hollow illusion. Charlotte didn't need the aetheric goggles hanging around her neck to know that any energy pulled out of his body would be of the most basic masculine frequency. Without the spiritual balls of an actual human, it didn't matter how big of a dick a Doll was sporting: it just wouldn't satisfy her real needs. Perhaps it was the playful irritation and possibility of failure that made actual people so much more satisfying, a spice of uncertainty that no machine could properly replicate. Just like sex itself, the struggle between multiple souls that melted into one was an aphrodisiac that no toy could quite get right. Although they'd had no luck in inventing a machine to completely replace actual men, those aviatrixes that tended toward the masculine end of the mystic spectrum were widely shunned and often went into voluntary exile among the grounders due to how they were treated, depriving the Matriarchy of a sympathetic source of male-polarity energy. Magic allowed no choice; either you used what was truly in your soul, or you had no more power than any other charlatan. No amount of reasoning or clever wordplay could change reality. You were who you were, and of all people tantric practitioners should have recognized that there was no malice or choice in the aviators' hearts. It was foolish and short-sighted to force them out, and Charlotte had come to verbal blows with the Matriarchy's ruling Crone Council more than once about their policies, both the explicit and the unspoken.

Unlike the relatively tiny Liberty Ships that would clamp onto the docking ring for resupply and recreation, the majority of Godmother was enclosed. Whether thinness of air or the comfort of a roof, the permanent inhabitants of the city preferred their homes and hallways enclosed, leading the Amethyst City to have an altogether claustrophobic air that Charlotte didn't much care for. Even growing up in the city she'd often climb out through windows and open doors, eager to sample the crisp air that the others didn't care for. She'd gotten more than her fair share of paddlings before the women charged with her care simply stopped fighting the girl's rebellious spirit.

A spirit that rose up in fiery fury at the idea that the crude gift of the Doll would somehow set things right between her and the cheating women who'd caused such heartache.

"Tell Erin if she wants to taste me so badly, she should come down here and beg herself, rather than sending a lollipop," Charlotte growled at the automaton, irritated with everything the artificial man represented, both societally and emotionally.

The Doll stared at her without comprehension as the aviatrix shoved his heavy frame off the docking ramp and through the open hatch into the enclosed city. He stumbled over the edge of the incline and into the shadows of the city's polished wooden corridor beyond, never once losing the beat on his pumping hand. His sad brass eyes made her almost pity Erin Enright. She truly had no comprehension of the damage she'd done if she thought the Doll would be gift enough to mend the fences.

Charlotte buried her face in her hands for a moment, fighting back the rage and pain. The boarding ramp was visible from windows along the docking ring, and she refused to let anyone see her breaking down. The work gloves' scent of engine oil, sweat, and leather helped the aviatrix center herself, although not as much as if she'd linked with the ship via the control ruby on her forehead. But these were her feelings, her emotions. She didn't want to numb them down; she wanted to burst through to the other side of them like a Liberty Ship through the storm clouds. There were still sunny skies ahead, but only if she braved the tempest head-on.

"ENGINEER FROST: IT IS UNWISE TO RESIST MAJOR ENRIGHT'S OVERTURES," a mechanical voice boomed through a speaker mounted on the outside of the docking ring, making Charlotte jump at the interruption of her brooding. The vox box was weathered and beaten by decades of exposure, making the words scratchy and interspersed with static.

"Crank the volume down a notch, Godmother," Charlotte snapped, slamming the city-ship's hatch shut and spinning the center wheel to seal it. She channeled a tiny amount of energy into the mechanism, accelerating rust already hiding within the gears with a boost. She nodded with satisfaction as she felt the gears lock; nobody else would be bothering her until it was repaired.

The outer docking ring stretched to both sides until it met city-sails at each end, with no sign of other aircraft. It was always relatively deserted, as Liberty Ships rarely returned except to refuel and to drop off new recruits whose eyes had been drawn to the skies. The boarding ramp creaked in protest from Charlotte's heavy footfalls as she stomped back to her ship. Although it was unlikely anyone would try to repair the hatch, winching the ramp back up felt good, as if no one could reach her, and the aviatrix relished the strain on her muscles as she worked the pulley. She set the brace on the upright boarding ramp, locking it in place and ensuring that there would be no more would-be gifts trying to board.

The only way over now was the worn docking clamp that still held the *Harlot's Promise* tight to the city, but even a fool wouldn't try their luck with the footing on the narrow steel surface. The beauty of the cloud-scattered open air, the sunset blazing on the ocean below, was all lost to her irritation even as the playful summer breeze tugged at her ponytail like a lover trying to jolly their mate out of a mood.

Even so, Godmother's static-filled voice easily carried over the distance, dogging the aviatrix like a hound on a fox.

"ENGINEER FROST—"

"Should have scrambled the speaker while I was at it!" Charlotte yelled, interrupting the crackling voice from the speaker. Knowing that Godmother was easily able to hear her even at this distance, the aviatrix took a deep breath, trying to compose herself. "And I told you to stop using titles when you address people. Makes you seem even less human than you are. Besides, ever since the split I'm also the only aviatrix on this Liberty Ship. Lauren has lost the right to call herself 'Captain' Frost; that's mine now. Whether I like it or not."

"VERY WELL. CAPTAIN FROST—"

"Stow it, Godmother," Charlotte said, cutting the vox box off again. "Fill the batteries and keep your opinions to yourself. I don't need your love advice, and I don't need a liar and cheater's Doll to fuck me over any more than I already am. I just want to get clear of her, of you, of this whole bloody place."

Silence reigned, the crack and pop of the speaker the only sounds in the air. Charlotte had often treated the artificial intelligence of Godmother with more kindness than other aviatrixes, but she wasn't in the mood to be chided by a mechanical busy-body.

The sentience that controlled the Matriarchy's city-ship was a strange amalgamation of human and machine, the intellect itself having arisen through the thirty years of sexual energy that had been generated to keep them aloft and out of the reaches of the rest of the world. The artificial intelligence was an unintended side effect of enhancing the industrial revolution with the sexual one, a surprise to all involved. At first there had been talk of purging the intellect from the floating city, but the Matriarchs had soon discovered that Godmother saw her creators as a family to be loved and protected, and her efforts had absolved the aviatrixes of the more mundane aspects of maintenance and navigation. What had started as a mindless marvel of technology and magic had become an overbearing mother hen that regarded the aviatrix citizens as her children.

"ERIN ONLY SEEKS YOUR FRIENDSHIP," Godmother squawked from the speaker, barely intelligible across the docking clamp, yet still irritating.

"No. She wants my pussy, my will…my forgiveness!" Charlotte shouted back, bitterness lacing her words. "She's not going to get any of them. Nor is Lauren. Not after what they did. They can both fuck right off."

Frost pulled the aetheric goggles over her eyes, shifting

the visual spectrum to see down through the wooden deck of the *Harlot's Promise*. The world was tinted amethyst by the crystal used to craft the lenses, but it allowed tantric engineers to work without having to constantly orgasm. While fun initially, such restrictions would exhaust even the most ardent practitioner eventually.

The light cedar planks of the deck faded from view, as did the interior support structure, leaving only the pulse of the eight accumulator batteries in the hold that powered the Liberty Ship. Energy glowed bright in four of them, but the others were barely receiving a trickle of tantric power from the city's reservoirs. While Charlotte and Lauren had kept the ship in the air during their travels, two people simply could not generate the kind of sexual energy that was needed for the long haul without more participants in the sexual festivities. But that was a scientific necessity; what Lauren had done with Erin was something altogether different.

"WERE YOU NOT RECEPTIVE TO OTHERS IN YOUR NEEDS? MONOGAMY IS NOT AN EFFICIENT USE OF YOUR SKILLS." The voice was louder now, more insistent.

"Lilith's tit, that's not the point!" Charlotte said, lowering the brass and leather aether goggles back down and trying not to scream in frustration again. She was getting hoarse with shouting at the city. The aviatrix lowered her voice to almost a whisper, barely audible to the waiting city-mind. "We could play with anyone, but we had to be open with each other. Lauren decided to fuck Erin behind my back and kept it secret, even after telling me she was done with her. A little extra spice, they said. No harm done, they said. But they both lied to my face. Multiple times."

"BUT DID YOU NOT ALSO—"

"Yes, for fuck's sake, yes!" Charlotte cried out, trying to shout down Godmother's voice. Her diminutive frame was nearly shaking with pent-up anger, an upwelling of betrayal the artificial intelligence was inadvertently stirring up. She knew she was losing control, but she didn't care anymore. Godmother wouldn't stop prodding, poking the pain of memory. "We all had fun that one time. But they kept going even after I asked Lauren, my *wife*, to stop seeing her! I asked, I begged Lauren to break it off with Erin. She agreed. But she lied, breaking the only rule that we had! Do you not understand that?"

"MAJOR ENRIGHT AND THE LEGION OF LILITH ARE A VITAL PART OF THE MATRIARCHY."

"That's not…that's not even the point…"

Charlotte was trying her best not to devolve into screaming at Godmother to just shut up. She'd been avoiding refueling for as long as she could to stave off this very situation. Godmother was trying to help, as she always had. Charlotte had lost her mother, one of the first Liberty captains, at a young age. The city's artificial intelligence had become the closest thing to a parent that the little girl had during her formative years, showing her the secret paths and hidden nooks within the superstructure that frustrated her assigned guardians. The Matriarchy had tried giving her to a foster family, but they couldn't keep their hands on the child long before the shadows of Godmother hid her again. Yet the more complicated human emotions and problems still eluded the city-mind no matter how beneficent her intentions, and sometimes it just hurt too much to teach her.

"I am well aware of the Legion's contributions," Charlotte said, willing the tears and pain down. She closed her eyes and evened out her breathing with a pranayama technique that helped to center her mind. The energies from the ship pulsed unseen at the edge of her senses, a soothing force that warmed her nether regions with tingles. When she was sure there were no more screams coming, she continued at a volume that would carry to the vox but not through the city walls.

"I'm also aware that they regard men as little more than mobile batteries that need to be either duplicated without souls or subjugated without mercy. Beyond sex, love, any of the other arguments against such brutality, there's also this one, simple fact: they're doing to men what was done to us for millennia. The Legion worship at the altar of superiority, not equality. If atrocities are Lilith's will, then that is a goddess I will not follow. And the Matriarchy shouldn't either. They're dangerous extremists that style themselves as our military using a mystic art form that is the antithesis of harming others. The very concept of a tantric soldier is as ridiculous as using sand as lubricant, and about half as effective."

Charlotte felt sick to her stomach at the thought of being watched by unseen eyes from the docking ring. She stalked down the stairs into the quarterdeck of the ship, disappearing within the *Harlot's Promise*. Although there was no escaping Godmother's prying attention, as the city-mind could hijack the ship's vox system, at least in the shadowed confines of the Liberty Ship the aviatrix could yell at the artificial busybody without making a complete spectacle of herself on the deck.

The cool air of the shadowed interior helped to soothe the hot anger that was building inside. The rich scarlet carpeting of this level of the ship was lush and deep; Charlotte sighed in contentment, letting the familiar comfort flow from her center to her extremities. She kicked off her heavy boots and socks, gripping the exquisite carpet with her toes and dropping her cable belt, chucking her work gloves after it. She'd been clambering around the outside of the ship doing maintenance when her would-be paramour showed up. By now in a normal visit to the Amethyst City she would generally be naked in a hot bath somewhere, perhaps even looking up a friend or three with Lauren. Due to the precepts of tantric magic a monogamous relationship was next to impossible to maintain, but marriage was still possible and exalted through a bond of trust. A few couples and polyfidelitous groups had managed it. Marriage between free peoples took work and honest communication, but it created something beautiful and precious, the kind of love that no storm or squall could sunder. Charlotte had believed Lauren, believed *in* her. They'd been inseparable in soul, love, and life.

Until the lies came to light.

Charlotte was less tolerant of other people's company now. The wound was just too fresh. It wasn't a good practice for any tantric aviatrix to shun couplings, let alone an engineer. Masturbation was fine and all, but the more people involved in the act the stronger the sexual energy generated. Even several monogamous couples working in tandem created a mystical field greater than any pair in isolation. But no matter the logic in finding another lover, Charlotte hadn't managed to get over the hurt Lauren had inflicted. So, the "wild child" the Legion had never managed to tame became even more isolated, fell even further to the fringes of the Matriarchy, became even more estranged from the only family she'd truly known.

Thinking of her ex-wife made the ship feel empty and hollow. They'd never been ones to take on a crew, and Liberty Ships rarely ran more than four or five aviatrixes anyway. But ever since they'd split, the lovely isolation the couple had once shared on the *Harlot's Promise* had left Charlotte as the only lady standing. Although she was perfectly capable of running the ship as both captain and engineer, it wasn't as much fun without a partner. The emptiness made Charlotte long for a distress call from the ground from one of the Matriarchy safe houses. A good old-fashioned midnight run of refugees seeking a new life was just the kind of heroic pick-me-up that would clear her head. But the signals from the ground agents had tapered off. A couple of decades of their smartest and fieriest girls fleeing unjust systems had forced the governments to start making changes that would entice them to stay. The old men in charge were sullen and selfish, but they also weren't clever enough to keep their wives and daughters from fleeing to the skies without changing their ways. And so long as Godmother floated above their weapon ranges, they were powerless to deny the superiority of the Matriarchy's technology.

Charlotte wandered over to one of the wide viewports that ran along the length of the *Harlot's Promise*, luxuriating in the dazzling amount of pure sunlight. The glass had been alchemically treated, but even the most advanced techniques couldn't make it any stronger than seasoned hardwood. Charlotte and Lauren had been admonished by the more paranoid ladies in the military, but they'd refused to live their lives shivering in fear. The glass was tough enough, especially since the *Harlot's Promise* wasn't a warship. With the maneuverability and landing options available to the airships, there'd been no need for weapons. A Liberty Ship came and went with only a whisper of its propellers to mark its passage, its magic-powered engines far quieter than any steam contraption. Still, there had been talk among the militant order of the Matriarchy, the Legion of Lilith, of developing actual weapons past the tantric stunners they had, debasing the Art by turning it to harm. The voices everywhere on Godmother were becoming more hawkish, angrier. Patience was wearing thin with the snail's-pace of change of the world, and the clouds did nothing to remind the aviatrixes of the humanity of ground-bound folk.

A gentle chime from the speakers sounded insistently. Charlotte grimaced.

"I said 'no,' Godmother. Whatever crocodile-tear message she is delivering now, tell Erin to shove it up her ass. Maybe Lauren can help dig it out after."

Unlike the exterior vox of the docking ring, the well-maintained ship speakers were free of static, able to communicate the concerned confusion of the city-mind.

"YOUR JEALOUSY IS ILLOGICAL. ALTHOUGH IT IS TRUE THAT THEY VIOLATED THE ACCORDS OF YOUR AGREEMENT, YOU ARE ALL STILL ON THE SAME SIDE. BUT AS YOU WISH. I AM TRANSMITTING A MORE POLITE REJECTION TO THE MAJOR. TANTRIC FEEDS INTO YOUR BATTERIES WILL BE INCREASED TO ALLOW SOONER DEPARTURE."

It hurt too much to smile over the small victory, so instead Charlotte gazed out at the amazing sight of a cloud-shrouded world. Godmother was currently floating a mile above the coastal border of the Ottoman Empire, giving Liberty Ships easy access Constantinople. Sultan Abdulaziz had continued his father and brother's reforms, giving equality to Muslim and non-Muslim people in the Levant region. But there were nationalist threats that were destabilizing the Sultan's rule, and as the Western nations soured and balked at the threat of the Matriarchy and of an independent sisterhood, so too had the Ottomans. And the Empire's recent brutal suppression of a rebellion in occupied Bulgaria had shown that they were still vulnerable to the same fears and mistakes as any other European nation.

After the first tantric engineers managed to launch the city twenty years ago grounders had gone a little crazy in regard to women, vowing that their wives and daughters would never join the debauched ranks of the Matriarchy, and cracking down hard on people who'd had little to no freedom to start with. Ironically, it was a woman, Queen

Victoria in Britain, who had become the Matriarchy's most vocal detractor. Although the queen was opposed to openly violent action against the aviatrixes, she was rumored to have turned a blind eye to the machinations of her subjects to bring down Godmother. The status quo had served Queen Victoria well, and her recalcitrance at recognizing the Matriarchy as a sovereign nation had been instrumental forcing them to live as wandering nomads of the skies. Although the Matriarchy tolerated grounder bigotry to a certain extent, it was out of necessity more than understanding. Beyond trading for supplies and other such things they could not produce in the sky, there was a simple matter of numbers. There were nearly two thousand free citizens aboard Godmother, along with their various children, playthings, and Dolls, as well as eleven Liberty Ships and their assorted crews who came and went as the winds called.

The world had everyone else.

Although the weapons in 1856 hadn't posed much problem for the first aviatrixes, the empires of man had been hard at work in the last two decades trying to figure out how to bring the Matriarchy down. They were getting closer each day, and the recent ballooner flights out of Europe had been heavily armed and surprisingly effective, forcing Godmother out of their airspace. They weren't quite producing airships yet, but they were damn close, and their mastery of artillery had become a real threat to the Amethyst City. While the Matriarchy held tight to the secrets of magic-augmented technology, the grounders' purely mechanical engineering was catching up at a frightening pace. The Legion could have held their former location over European territory only at the cost of a massacre on both sides. One of the factions had to show some modicum of common sense, and as usual it was the women who'd chosen not to sacrifice life just to rattle sabers. Besides, the Crone Council had agents infiltrated throughout the land; the hope was that equality could be brought about without bloodshed if they were just patient.

Below Charlotte the beautiful deep-blue Mediterranean Sea surged gently against the shoreline, the surf barely visible as a white froth where it crashed against the land. Farther inland, mountains covered with vegetation blocked much of the view of the arid lands beyond. To the starboard of the *Harlot's Promise* there was open water, but that was where the danger approached from. Specks on the ocean horizon were all that she could see of the Ottoman Navy so far, but the ships the Sultan had worked so hard to modernize were already steaming toward Godmother's position, eager to try the range of their cannon. Although the Matriarchy had chosen to avoid hovering directly over major cities in case the governments had put aside their differences to bring down the "uppity women," it seemed as if simply existing was reason enough for jealous grounders to try their luck at downing the city-ship. The treasure trove of forbidden sexual technology was a powerful lure to those who coveted power.

"Godmother: query. What is the status of the Ottoman infiltration?"

There was a crackle of the ship's speakers as the city processed Charlotte's request and security level. Although aviatrixes were supposedly all equal in the Matriarchy, the Crones were by their nature predisposed to secrets. The Council was made up of the best minds from the first generation of tantric engineers, the city-builders, and their desperate efforts to construct the mighty Godmother had necessitated a certain amount of paranoia that was not easily shaken off. They were wont to compartmentalize information, a holdover from the methods that kept them safe in the old days.

"EARLY ANALYSIS INDICATES THAT THE MATRIARCHY WILL TAKE CONTROL OF THE GOVERNMENT WITHIN THE MONTH VIA THE SEDUCTION OF SULTAN ABDULAZIZ."

"It's just so stupid," Charlotte said, shaking her head at the situation. "The whole place is a powder keg, and the religious nationalists already hate the Sultan with a passion. If it's discovered he's under the sway of one of our agents, I fear the response. There's a good chance one of the more conservative imams will get a bee in his bonnet and lead a revolution. There'd be a lot of blood spilled, win or lose. As much as I hate their close-minded attitudes, ignorance shouldn't be punished by civil war. How much bloodshed can we justify in our self-righteous meddling? Is it really so difficult for the Matriarchy to show patience, to allow us time to effect peaceful change with the Liberty Ships? The Sultan is proof positive that the governments of man have begun to show glimmers of hope and humility. Once they find out we're manipulating them behind the scenes though, they will never accept peace. Where do we go from there?"

Godmother was silent. For her, the question had no

relevance. The Crone Council had already decided, and events had been set in motion. The Matriarchy had never been this bold before; it was unsettling how little resistance there had been among the citizens to the idea of such an infiltration and direct control. The first generation that had raised the city into the sky remembered fathers and sons, husbands and brothers, men who they'd loved even in the face of what history had taught women about pain. But no adult males lived on Godmother, and the law was that once a boy came of age the mother had to either find him a home on the surface or to leave with him. Many had chosen to settle back on the surface, bringing revolutionary ideas with them. Though the rule kept the Matriarchy safe, it had unintentionally given rise to a generation of women who'd never known a man except as a servant or conquered lover. Thus, patience moved to haste. And knowledge moved to ignorance.

The Legion infiltrators had worked hard at cultivating local contacts and preparing for the silent war, using Godmother's calculations and advice to move their plans. But if they pushed too hard too fast the fragile scaffolding of the future would collapse back into savagery. The Matriarchy had its proponents among the people of the Ottoman Empire but just like in the west, the men in charge were frightened and suspicious, using Allah as Europeans had used God to justify their oppression. No matter the shade of skin or belief system, those in power knew that invoking divine mandate was an excellent way of quelling rebellious thought. And the recent atrocities against Bulgaria stood as a warning that violence was still the easiest tool for the Ottomans to reach for. It didn't help that people who might have otherwise supported revolutionary ideas were regarded as inferior and untrustworthy by most of the Matriarchy. The aviatrixes had lived too long in the clouds and were too used to looking down on everyone else, both literally and figuratively.

Sirens suddenly began shrieking aboard Godmother, loud enough to be heard across the intervening distance from the docking ring and within the *Harlot's Promise* itself, setting Charlotte's teeth to rattling.

"Really, Godmother?" she shouted. "What could warrant that sound level?"

The ship's speaker crackled with soft static, but no voice piped up to explain the commotion. Godmother's formidable attention was concentrated somewhere else, piquing the aviatrix's curiosity.

Charlotte shoved her feet back into the boots and pelted up the stairs and out on to the deck as an explosion somewhere on the city-ship rumbled through the docking clamp to the *Harlot's Promise*. Charlotte heard shots ring out inside the docking ring, and her eyes widened in surprise. They were using actual firearms, not stunners.

"Godmother! Answer me! What's going on?"

Still the artificial intelligence remained silent. Charlotte debated lowering the boarding ramp and undogging the city's outer hatch. But before her curiosity could get the better of her common sense the docking hatch shuddered on its hinges from a sudden impact on the other side. Desperate pounding sounded for a moment, and then the hatch wheel began to spin, grinding the mystically advanced rust to dust as the mechanism was forced. Gunshots rang out followed by a cry of pain.

Captain Charlotte Frost took a reflexive step back, waiting with bated breath for the hatch to open. More firearm shots rang out in the docking corridor before being drowned out by a hair-raising inhuman shriek from the thing on the other side of the hatch.

There was a monster rampaging in the city, and it was coming right for her.

Chapter 2

Suddenly the twenty feet of open air between the ship and the docking ring didn't feel that far. Although the boarding ramp wasn't down, Charlotte was keenly aware of the clamp holding the Liberty Ship hostage. Even though it was a four-foot drop from the city's outer hatch to the slick steel of the clamp, and a deadly fall if you missed, now it didn't look as impossible as it had a few minutes ago. Whatever monster the other aviatrixes were chasing might find it no more impossible than someone leaping over a small puddle. What danger would the half-mile fall on either side of the narrow brace matter to whatever had just wrenched the gears free of the rust and had the city passing out firearms to stop?

"Godmother, cut the docking clamp! Let my ship go!" Charlotte shouted in alarm, stroking the smooth cool surface of the gem in her forehead to initiate the mental link.

The small ruby augmented her ajna chakra, sending thoughts to the control console that rested safely within the confines of the quarterdeck. The captain reached out with her senses into the ship's central system, sending a pulse of willpower down to the analytics core to wake it up. Difference engines throughout the *Harlot's Promise* sprang into action, transmitting her consciousness throughout the ship's frame. The seaward and skyward masts shuddered as they extended like a startled lizard's frill from the hull above and below, drawing taut the white canvas sails of the steering fins. Stored magic surged from the batteries to the pontoon engines, and the giant propellers began to turn, ready to spin up to cruising speed.

The *Harlot's Promise* was eager to soar away, but she was still held tightly to Godmother by the unreleased docking mechanism. It was a simple affair, essentially just a large steel clamp that was sturdy enough to hold an unpowered airship indefinitely for repairs and refuel. But there was a price to be paid for giving Liberty Ships a rest within its clutches: there was no freedom to be had unless Godmother released the docking clamp. If Charlotte tried to force her ship free the *Harlot's Promise* would be torn apart by the efforts.

The docking speaker crackled, heavy with static. "CAPTAIN FROST: DEPARTURE IS NOT AUTHORIZED. PLEASE STAND BY FOR LEGION FORCES TO TAKE CONTROL OF YOUR SHIP AND SITUATION."

"The fuck they will!" Charlotte shouted back. But it was an empty denial; without Godmother's permission Charlotte wasn't going anywhere.

With a loud clang the city's docking hatch was shoved open, the steel door smashing back against its hatches with a surprising amount of force. The din of battle was suddenly released from the confined hall into the open air by the open, screams and gunfire punctuating the danger.

But what emerged from the shadowed dock hallway brought all of Charlotte's fears to a confused halt.

The "monster" the other aviatrixes were chasing was the most elaborate Doll that Charlotte had ever seen.

Female in form, the construct was built like a mythical Amazon, six feet tall with a well-muscled frame with the customary lack of hair that all mechanicals shared. But the ivory plates that served as the majority of her body was far better sculpted than anything Charlotte had ever seen, with delicate curves and cuts that beggared belief. More than that though, arcane patterns of silver filigree ran through the plates, almost imperceptible save for when the afternoon's fading light caught it, weaving tantric formulae of incomprehensible complexity that moved and changed with the Doll's motions. Whereas brass and tin were the base materials used for the moving parts of a normal automaton this strange construct instead had golden cogs and gears visible through the translucent skin that covered the joints. The Doll's eyes were featureless orbs of gold, and her lips were lushly detailed in the same precious materials. The automaton's face was the most perfect sculpture Charlotte had ever seen, even contorted in pain as it was.

The rest of the Doll's body was exquisitely sculpted as well; whereas a normal automaton had only the most basic of sexual organs with the occasionally artistic flair, this particular one went beyond anything the aviatrix had thought possible, from the lifelike golden nipples of the large breasts to the astonishingly detailed genitals. The slit of the Doll's sex peeked demurely from her pubic mons, tempting exploration with its promise of the gentle warmth within. For a moment Charlotte couldn't help imagining her fingers running across the soft ivory skin down to the secrets within as the Doll gasped in ecstasy. The aviatrix felt her need rising like a steaming volcano on the edge of eruption, rumbling urges she hadn't experienced since Lauren's betrayal.

Marring the Doll's beauty however was a bullet hole in her right thigh, where sparks of violet energy were flashing as she bled out raw tantric energy.

"Pardon me, madam. My eyes are up here," the Doll remarked with a dry grin, making Charlotte realize that she'd been staring at the artificially perfect frame and modifications, lost in the unexpected fantasies of ravishing the animated sculpture before her. The automaton's voice was strong, carrying over the intervening distance clearly.

Charlotte flushed like a virgin caught in the first tentative groping.

"Yes, well, the boarding ramp is also up, here," Charlotte countered, hooking a thumb to the side at the locked winch that held the ramp upright, trying to cover her embarrassment.

"Yes, I see that," the Doll said, humor lacing her words. She began to inch out onto a small ledge that ran the length of the docking ring, moving herself out of the line of fire from inside, opposite of where the hatch had smashed into the ring. The wind buffeted her, and she swayed, clinging precariously with fingertips and feet to walls never meant for it. Every movement of the beautiful Doll was an expression of elegance, but it was only a matter of time until a gust made her lose her footing and plunge to her death. "Could I, perhaps, impress upon the exalted aviatrix before me to lower my means of ingress? The soldiers chasing me are rather insistent on violence."

From within the hidden confines of the enclosed docking ring a voice rang out that made Charlotte grit her teeth in frustrated rage.

"Intruder, power down and surrender yourself!" Major Erin Enright yelled, her voice echoing down the corridor. The Major was playing it safe, making sure that she kept her women back and taking her time.

"Of course, it had to be her," Charlotte muttered, too low to be heard by even the Doll. "Of all the fucking people, it *had* to be her."

Although there was precious little ledge for the Doll's feet to shuffle on, an impotent shot rang out from the docking hallway, encouraging her to slide as far away from the opening as she could.

"She's trying to get herself on the Frost ship!" Erin shouted from inside the docking ring. Every word made Charlotte's temper rise higher. She still hadn't seen the Major, but she imagined the soldier and her security team were arrayed around their side of the docking hatch, trying to get a bead on the errant automaton.

The Doll inched out onto the narrow ledge, back to the wall with hands desperately sliding over the smooth surface seeking purchase. It was a miracle she hadn't already fallen. The wind a half mile up was fickle, and at any moment an angry gust could send the automaton tumbling into a deadly fall. Nothing could survive from this height, least of all a machine with such delicate clockwork. Even now, the wind was rising, threatening to pluck the Doll off the side of the docking ring and send her down to her doom.

"It would appear that sooner would be better than later," the Doll called out, fear writ large over her face.

"That sounds like a really stupid thing for me to do," Charlotte yelled back over the wind. Although she'd dearly love to tweak Erin's nose by spiriting her prey away, she was no fool. The Doll was dangerous enough that the Major and her forces were using firearms and keeping their distance. Charlotte enjoyed taking risks, but there was a sharp bell of self-preservation ringing.

"Please," the Doll pleaded, her voice soft and earnest. "My memories are jumbled, but I am certain they wish to use me to inflict great harm. This is not a destiny I wish."

Charlotte stared at her in disbelief. "You're a sex toy. Not a weapon."

Even as she said it, though, the aviatrix doubted her own words. There was something about this overly-intricate automaton, the too-lifelike responses, the self-awareness, that disturbed the captain.

"Char, babe!" Erin shouted from the corridor. She was creeping closer by the sound of her voice. "Keep your distance! That thing'll kill you if it don't enslave you first!"

"Fuck you, asshole!" Charlotte screamed back, raising a middle finger at the unseen Major. Every word out of the woman's mouth made Charlotte's resolve against the Doll quaver. Whatever the machine was, recovering it was important to Erin.

It would be nice to see the almighty Major lose something for once.

"I cannot, I will not, go back," the Doll stated with a stoic look. "There is only one way forward for me now."

The wounded automaton crouched down; her gaze locked on the chipped yellow paint of the docking clamp. It was a good three feet down from the tiny ledge she clung to; if she faltered or missed, the only thing below the clamp was thin air and a long fall.

"I wouldn't," Charlotte warned, despite herself.

The Doll looked up, locking her with golden eyes. Charlotte felt as if the machine was weighing her mind and soul. The ghost of a smile crossed the lifelike lips.

"For freedom? Yes. Yes, I believe you would."

With those words the Doll dropped down with uncanny grace to the docking clamp. Her aim was excellent, but the wounded leg collapsed under her weight. She gave a small cry of distress as her feet slipped out from under her but managed to topple forward instead of to the side, landing front-first on the narrow beam and wrapping her arms around it to steady herself. Charlotte fought back the need to help her; it was getting harder and harder to ignore the machine's plight, no matter how much common sense kept justifying it. There was something innocent, something pure, in how certain the Doll was about herself and the situation.

Struggling upright, the swaying Doll managed to get to her feet again. The slick beam of the clamp made for poor footing, and the automaton nearly fell as she struggled to balance on the curved surface. The docking mechanism was only a few inches wide, and the frequent breezy gusts were heavy enough to make the elegant Doll's footing unsure, her bountiful chest heaving in terror. The mechanical's face, as intricate and nuanced as a living person, was etched tight with pain and panic in equal measure.

"Are you insane?" Charlotte asked, her breath catching in her throat at every sway, every step that could easily spell doom for the determined automaton. Despite her protestations, she found herself silently cheering the machine on.

"I…I told you," the Doll said, her balance swaying with her words. "I am not going back."

"You don't get that choice, vacant," came a snarl from the docking ring's hatch.

Major Erin Enright was braced against the hatch frame with a rifle in her hand centered on the Doll. Like other Legionnaires, she wore a Greco-styled deep green armored skirt with a breastplate of polished steel. The Major's uniform included a single pauldron with her rank inscribed on the shoulder, with a pair of black gloves and boots rounding out the uniform. Erin was a big woman, well over six feet tall with broad shoulders, and she favored a short cut for her flaming red hair. Freckles sprayed across her nose and ran across her muscled arms and thighs. Memories of their one shared night overwhelmed Charlotte, to quickly be replaced by the imagination of Erin and Lauren curled together, laughing at Charlotte, lying right to her face.

Captain Frost felt her blood run hot, her temper rising like a dragon in her veins.

The Major raised the rifle to her shoulder, aiming at the unsteady Doll swaying on the docking clamp. It was an easy killshot, not even ten feet away. Erin was taking her time, enjoying the helpless position of her prey.

"I got you cold," she sneered at the Doll. "Toddle your pretty little ass back here. Godmother said to take you alive, but I'm good either way after what you did."

Charlotte saw the ugly meanness that the major had let out before, that same deaths-head grin that the thought of torturing men had elicited from her. She was the woman who gave truth to what the grounders believed about the Matriarchy, the worst instincts and inequalities distilled into a vengeful spirit. Abusers often dreamt up their opponents with traits that mirrored them, and Erin was that dream given form. Instead of the glorious promise that the Liberty Ships represented, she was the subjugation, the humiliation, the sins of the world with a different flavor, but justified the same way. It would so easy to fall under that spell, to succumb to the propaganda that somehow their own hatred was any more noble than the ones they'd fought against for generations. In Erin, Charlotte saw all that was wrong with the Legion and the Matriarchy, a festering rot of supremacy and exclusion.

The Doll froze in place, arms outstretched as she balanced on the steel clamp.

"There is much you do not know," the automaton stated, not turning around to face Erin. "There is much I do not, either. And I fear that you, who are so quick to follow orders you do not comprehend, will not allow such investigations."

The Major lowered her rifle, her confusion obvious.

"I will not return," the Doll said. Her golden gaze bore into Charlotte's heart, pleading, begging. The aviatrix stood at the crossroads, and she felt the scales weighing, balancing. The automaton was only a few feet away now, having crossed much of the distance with her unsteady gait.

"Don't make me do it, vacant," Erin warned, her voice low and dangerous as she raised the rifle back up. "And you stay out of this, Char. Final warning."

The Doll leapt forward to the promise of freedom.

Aiming for the *Harlot's Promise* railing that Charlotte was leaning against, the Doll's wounded leg robbed her leap of most of its power. She cried out, the empty air below inviting her to death.

Charlotte lunged out and caught the Doll's flailing hand, hooking her feet around the railing as she jumped.

A shot rang out from the Major's rifle.

Somehow, even at only twenty feet away, the best shot in the Legion of Lilith missed.

The bullet threw out chips of wood from the ship's hull next to Charlotte's head, its passage so close that the aviatrix felt the breeze of its passing on her face.

Grunting with the effort, Charlotte held tight to the Doll as they dangled over the side of the ship. The aviatrix wrapped her feet around the railing as tightly as she could, but it creaked dangerously, as did the captain's arms. Her sockless feet felt slick and sweaty in the boots, and it was all too easy to imagine simply slipping out of them. Despite the beauty of the Doll, Charlotte couldn't help but fixate on the half mile fall beyond to the unforgiving ocean below.

Dangling helplessly, Charlotte's legs were already on fire. Even with the mystical alterations that helped Dolls weigh less than their components, the intricate automaton was a hundred pounds or so, and the aviatrix was not strong enough to hold the precarious position for long. Charlotte felt stretched out, both arms clinging desperately to the beautiful machine.

A sharp crack split the air as Erin fired again from across the gap, hitting the Doll in her unwounded leg, eliciting a shocked cry from the automaton. Even with the burning of her muscles and the fall threatening them, Charlotte couldn't understand how the markswoman hadn't simply gunned them both down.

"Char, let that thing go!" Erin ordered, cussing between every word. She was still safely kneeling in the hatchway of the docking ring as she chambered another bullet in her rifle. "I don't want to kill you both. But I will."

"Please," the Doll whispered, golden eyes wide in fear. "Please, do not drop me."

"I can't...my feet are slipping..." Charlotte gasped, trying to keep her grip on the Doll. The aviatrix felt her ankles bruising and twisting on the rail from the weight, feet shifting in her boots dangerously. If she held on much longer, they were both going to die.

"Then...do you wish to be free?" the Doll asked, dangling from the captain's grip. She slackened her hold on Charlotte's hand, the unspoken offer of a life for a life.

Instead of letting her go, the aviatrix pulled her closer, muscles screaming from the motion.

"I don't give up," Charlotte growled, her arms burning in protest.

A fleeting smile of relieved surprise crossed the Doll's perfect face before being replaced by a sad resolve.

"Then I believe this may help, Captain. Please forgive me for the impertinence."

The Doll reached down between her dangling legs with her free hand, gently rubbing fingers across her smooth pussy before slipping them up and touching her perfectly nestled clit ever so briefly as she bit her lower lip in excitement. There was an exotic scent in the air, like lilacs in a fresh spring field, and Charlotte felt her pulse quicken in response. Before the aviatrix could object, the Doll reached up and ran her glistening fingers across the skin of Charlotte's hands.

The touch was like a live wire, a high voltage shock that ran up Charlotte's arm and into her body. For a moment it felt as if she would give everything for the Doll, do anything for her, as the sexual venom penetrated her skin. Instinctually, Charlotte pulled a burst of tantric energy from the ship's batteries, empowering her muscles, and the physical strain of the automaton's weight vanished.

Charlotte began to swing back and forth, her foothold on the railing now as stable as a steel ring. Without any appreciable effort, the captain swung both herself and the Doll up and over the railing. Distantly, in the back of her mind, the aviatrix could feel that she'd torn muscles. But it didn't seem to matter. Nothing mattered, not pain, not fear. Only the beauteous automaton that stood before her.

Her head still reeling from the intoxicant, Charlotte was unable to resist when the automaton reached up to her face and gently rubbed still-glistening fingers gently across the aviatrix's lips.

"I am so sorry," the Doll whispered. "But I cannot allow them to enslave me. Please, mistress.

"Save me."

The taste of the automaton's sex was like nothing Charlotte had ever experienced before. Although she tended to be more attracted to men, the aviatrix had loved many ladies before. The heady moisture of the Doll lacked the musky taste of a natural woman's excitement, instead tingling against the captain's senses like a bolt of lightning caught within the sweet nectar of luscious honey. It was overwhelming, and Charlotte felt her senses stripped away with the primal urge to throw the Doll to the ground and ravish her. The aviatrix throbbed with a deep need as she pressed herself against the automaton, pulling the machine's elegantly-sculpted head in for a hungry kiss that stole their shared breath. The weight from the Doll's disabled legs didn't exist for Charlotte as she held the machine close, passion raging within her breast.

"Char, what the fuck are you doing?" Erin shouted in alarm. Her voice came to Charlotte as if from the end if a long tunnel, irritating and brash but distant.

Warning shots impacted into the railing next to the entwined pair. Distantly Charlotte heard Erin call out to the other legionnaires crowding the docking hatch frame to hold their fire. Somewhere in the tingling sensation of her clouded universe Charlotte could swear the Major was pleading with her to let the Doll go, to get away from the dangerous automaton. But it didn't matter; nothing mattered except her need, her craving.

The Doll's golden lips and tongue were remarkably soft and smooth, carrying a different taste than her vital juices, but just as addictive, and as skilled in technique as any tantric engineer. They played over Charlotte's mouth, nibbling, loving, softly exploring and caressing.

"I can show you how to release yourself, Captain," the Doll breathed into their kiss.

Charlotte's body was rigid with need, her erect nipples pushing painfully against the snug flight leathers. It was all she could do to stop her hands from ripping off her clothes and fall to pleasuring herself, but somewhere a spark of survival rose up, fighting to clear her head.

The Doll stroked the side of Charlotte's face, reaching up as her fingers twirled near the captain's temple. A faint glittering current of modulated magic flowed from the machine's fingertips into the captain's mind. A ghostly sequence of numbers and letters formed in the aviatrix's thoughts.

Charlotte closed her eyes and reached out to the *Harlot's Promise*, extending her will aetherically through the ship's systems like a possessing phantom. The network of libidium-laced steel carried her consciousness through the airship like blood in the veins, waking the Liberty Ship from her slumber. Despite not having a fully-developed consciousness like Godmother, any tantrically-imbued vessel carried mystical echoes of the souls that fueled it, soaked into wood and steel. The longer a Liberty Ship was piloted by the same crew, the more of a personality it began to develop. For over two years, the only interface the *Harlot's Promise* had felt was from the Frost wives, and she had coalesced a stronger thrum of intelligence than normal as a result. But now there was an absence, a deep ache that mirrored Charlotte's own at the loss of Lauren. Although not aware enough to understand why, the ship could still feel the void where her other aviatrix should have been.

The physical thrall of the Doll's sexual venom on Charlotte was drastically reduced by the captain's link, allowing the aviatrix to think clearly enough to realize something startling: what was affecting her was no mere chemical reaction. The sexual venom was imbued with tantric magic, a faint insidious glow that laced it like arsenic hidden in drink.

Charlotte opened her eyes, and the world had stabilized. She could feel the Doll's mind control cocktail at the edge of her will, but as long as the ajna ruby connected her with the *Harlot's Promise*, she was able to ignore its soporific effect on her body. Distantly Charlotte noted the pain from the torn muscles that had resulted from her hoisting the Doll onboard that her muddled senses had been masking. It was a simple thing to augment her body with the magic from the batteries, and the aviatrix accelerated her healing as a result. She'd be sore later, but it was a small price to pay. Charlotte shifted the Doll against her body, leaning against the railing to take some of the weight off.

The Doll's eyes widened in surprise, her face naked

with fear. She had realized that Charlotte had broken free of her control.

"CAPTAIN FROST: DO NOT ASSIST THE CONSTRUCT. SHE IS A DANGEROUS WEAPON AND WILL DESTROY YOU."

"Listen to Godmother, Char!" the Major shouted.

Charlotte locked Erin's eyes with a fiery glare across the dangerous gap, channeling all of the hurt and betrayal as she transmitted the docking release code that the Doll had given her through the ship and its link with the city.

"My name is Charlotte," she snarled, her mind clear, her will strong and fiery. "Not 'Char.' Not 'babe.' Not 'stupid trusting bitch.'

"*Captain* Charlotte Fucking Frost," the aviatrix spat.

The docking clamp released with a loud clang, and the *Harlot's Promise* leapt away from Godmother. The Doll was a warm, comforting weight in the captain's arms. The situation made her feel as a knight, spiriting the fair maiden away from the clutches of a dragon. Charlotte smirked with satisfaction at Erin's shocked and hurt expression before turning her back on the Major.

Turbulence had already begun to pick up from their acceleration; although the flight aura would reduce both it and inertia to some extent, there was still a danger of a sudden crosswind being enough to pluck an unwary aviatrix from the deck like a grape from a vine. Even as she directed her body to descend the stairs into the carpeted quarterdeck Charlotte's mind flowed within the *Harlot's Promise*, adjusting for aetheric currents as naturally as a bird taking wing.

Through the instrument clusters running the length of the *Harlot's Promise* that served as her senses Charlotte bore witness to the Amethyst City's impressive glory as they soared away. For the grounders, the flying city was a cloud-enshrouded myth given form, a fairy tale castle in the sky. The fading sunlight glittered over her libidium walls, and there was a pang of regret in the aviatrix's heart. Godmother was so much more to her than a home. But the artificial mother had raised Charlotte to believe in herself, to believe in her values and standards. She only hoped Godmother would see that, and that somewhere in the depths of the city's soul, that she would even be proud of her.

Charlotte tucked the *Harlot's Promise* into a southern heading, bringing them level as they sped along the rocky surf between ocean and land. As her senses returned more to her body, the captain realized she was still feeling the effects from the potent venom she'd been drugged with. A hot flash of anger cut through the euphoria, and Charlotte held on to it as she centered her mind.

The Doll was nuzzling into her, sighing in relief at not being handed over. Charlotte broke the embrace, gently but firmly pushing the confused automaton to the handrail that ran around the anteroom's wall. Even with the rail's assistance, the Doll's injured legs refused to support her. Charlotte helped the automaton lower herself to the floor. She sat demurely with her pale legs together. Even so, the top of her labia peeked out, an alluring beacon that was difficult to ignore. The Doll gave a grateful look to Charlotte, her hands lingering on the aviatrix's arms, as soft and firm as promises on a lover's lips. The captain vacillated between angry and turned on, but an alert from the ship's sensors demanded her attention.

Four small specks detached themselves from Godmother like bats from a roost and angled directly toward the fleeing Liberty Ship. Charlotte dialed the sensors in closer and saw spherical orbs of wood and runed steel, canvas sails on each side that fluttered like insect wings in the wind. Enforcers, remote-controlled security flitters about the size of a person. Each bore on its belly the only weapon the tantric engineers had ever designed: an energy lance that could bypass armor and stun the victim with a quivering orgasm that would leave them unable to form coherent thought for a time. Although the enforcer flitters were fragile, they had the advantage of speed and maneuverability, able to overtake the *Harlot's Promise* with ease. Even though it would take an extraordinarily lucky shot to hit Charlotte blind through the hull, the stun beams were also able to disrupt the flight auras of airships. Each shot they landed on the ascension field would feed more information to the remote flitters, until they could finally adjust their beam frequencies to collapse the field that kept the *Harlot's Promise* aloft. Without magic the Liberty Ship was no airworthier than any other brick, and Charlotte's survival chances would be somewhere between laughable and nonexistent.

"Now would be the time for explanations," the aviatrix sighed, pulling her consciousness out of the ship's frame. Somewhere in the back of her head Charlotte felt the tiny bit of her mind that was still connected to the *Harlot's Promise*, maintaining their course as they turned inland, away from the pursuing flitters. All aviatrixes learned the vital skill of partitioning their minds, but few were as capable at the skill as Charlotte. She was one of the three or four tantric engineers who could maintain basic navigation even during sleep. The presence of the Liberty Ship's personality echo made it even easier, as the vessel was eager to assist in her own course.

The Doll reached for her from the carpeted floor, eyes beseeching. Charlotte jumped back, causing a hurt expression to flit across the Doll's sculpted features.

"I'm getting really tired of people trying to control me," Charlotte growled. "You try that stunt again and the flitters won't have a chance to shoot us down. I'll slam this ship into the ground and laugh in your face as we burn. No one puts a leash on me."

"An impulse I well understand," the Doll said, using the handrail to reseat herself against the wall. The activity caused her to stretch her chest, making her bosom even more pronounced as they gently bobbed around. Charlotte couldn't help but think of the Liberty Ship's wardrobe, a massive collection of various cultural clothes and…other styles. The image of the Doll trying on the aviatrix's extensive collection of bustiers was somehow lewder and more exciting than the perfectly naked automaton in front of her.

The Doll smiled at noticing where Charlotte was staring. "Perhaps I will be allowed to make a proper apology?"

"Cut that shit out," Charlotte said, pulling from the strength of her link with the *Harlot's Promise* to put iron in her words and cold water over her smoldering lust. "Now explain to me, quickly, why I shouldn't let the flitters overtake us. You drugged me against my will in an attempt to seize control of my ship."

The Doll actually looked guilty, casting her gaze down in shame, picking at the edges of the bullet wounds in her legs nervously. Whoever had built the machine was a true artist, a mistress of tantric engineering with skill that Charlotte couldn't even begin to fathom. Beyond merely being physically perfect, the mysterious creator had managed to imbue the Doll with all the subtle and unspoken traits that gave her the illusion of life. The machine looked up at her, golden eyes filled with pain and uncertainty.

"Please. I seek asylum."

"A little late for 'please' and 'thank you', wouldn't you say?" Charlotte replied, but with a less acrid tone than before.

The Doll shook her head ruefully. "I am truly sorry. I did you a disservice. You chose to not drop me, and I rewarded your largesse by envenoming you. That I saw no other recourse in the moment does not absolve me of the sin."

Through the ship's sensors Charlotte noticed the enforcers getting closer. She could almost hear their weapons powering up.

"So, you *do* understand consent, then. Could've fooled me. Who are you seeking asylum from, anyway? The Matriarchy? Sugar, I hate to break it to you, but they turned you out from a machine shop, and there's no way any grounder will treat you as anything other than a sex toy or a demon. Hell, I'm liable as not to take you apart just to see how your builder managed such a convincing facsimile of human. You're wonderfully built, even by our standards."

"I...I am not sure you are correct," the Doll said.

Charlotte gave a short, sharp laugh. "Are you serious? I've never seen a model as advanced as you."

"No," the Doll shook her head. "You do not take my meaning. An echo of a memory, a whisper of the past, tells me that the people I was running from had no hand in my birth."

"Now I see why they were shooting at you. Are dangerous delusions part of your malfunction?"

"Please believe me," the Doll pleaded. "By my life, I swear to you that I know I was born, not built. I am no machine."

"I hate to be the one to tell you, but that's exactly what you are," Charlotte said, shrugging uneasily. "An automaton, a Doll, a construct without soul or mind. Any semblance of consciousness you possess is just a clever engineer or a particularly potent batch of tantric energy that you were infused with. You're not alive; you're just really good at faking it."

"You seem so certain." There was a hint of a smile on the Doll's face. The beautiful curve of her lush lips promised naughty things, but the captain's link to the *Harlot's Promise* reinforced her will. "As you can personally attest I...feel... very real."

Charlotte shrugged, trying to keep her fingertips from twitching with the desire to touch the Doll. "Look, I'm sure you believe you're a real person, Pinocchio. And I've got to admit, whoever put you together went above and beyond. But you're nothing but an illusion of gold and ivory given motion."

"No," the Doll repeated firmly, her hands moving over her naked body in a way that made the captain's face flush. "I feel, I *know*, that you are in error. You must use better eyes than the others…mistress."

Charlotte's heart fluttered at the demure way the Doll used the word, full of unspoken pleasures. But the machine's insistence did make her curious as to what its aura looked like. Most automatons had miniscule halos, nothing compared to even the dullest human. The aviatrix pulled her aetheric goggles up over her eyes. The world of the physical dissolved around her, leaving only energy flows of both magical and mundane forces, a strange abstract world of color and feeling like a watercolor painting in the rain. Turning her altered sight on the Doll caused Charlotte's heart to skip a beat.

The Doll was alive.

Truly, utterly alive. Rather than the dim flicker of the artificially-infused energy others of her ilk demonstrated, the Doll's mystical nadi veins were blazing with light, almost too bright to stand, as was the power of her aura. Not only was the automaton's energy equal to a living being, but she was actually exceeding any Charlotte had ever viewed before. Even tantric engineers were not infused with so much, relying more on their synthesized technology to interact with the magic. The captain had no idea how the machine's creators had managed it, but somehow the Doll had been infused with so much tantric energy that she'd achieved true life and consciousness, beyond that of even Godmother herself.

"I am Tash," the Doll stated, as Charlotte lowered her goggles. The impression of overwhelming power lingered though.

"Charlotte," the aviatrix replied, nodding her head cautiously. "I'd say nice to meet you, but in polite society we generally don't force our fingers into someone else's mouth after touching our pussies. It's considered slightly uncouth without asking first. Would really break up a proper tea party if the ladies greeted each other like that."

A rueful smile crawled across the Doll's face.

"Attention, Liberty Ship *Harlot's Promise*," the internal speakers crackled. Although Godmother was controlling the combat flitters, it was Erin's voice that was being transmitted. "Char. Charlotte. Please. You have no idea what's onboard with you. It's more dangerous than you can possibly imagine. We need it back, and there's no room for arguments. I...I really don't want to do this, babe. But if you don't turn around and bring the Doll back, we'll be forced to open fire. Please. If this is about Lauren, we can talk—"

With a grimace Charlotte cut the feed, quieting the speakers.

"They're going to shoot us down. Peachy," Charlotte muttered. She arched a quizzical eyebrow at the Doll. "So. Tash. Not that I'm going to help you, but for argument's sake, and because it'll piss off Erin, why exactly are they so eager to get you back?"

"It is simple, Captain Frost," the construct replied gravely. "They need me to destroy the world."

Chapter 3

Charlotte laughed out loud.

"Are delusions of grandeur part of your original programming, or a recent development?" the aviatrix asked.

In a very human gesture of frustration, the Doll sighed heavily and ran her palm over her face. "Why must you doubt the evidence right before your eyes? Think on it, mistress. Work through the implications. You will arrive at the same destination I did."

Her tone brought Charlotte up short, and her giggles petered out. But the thoughts that nibbled at the edge of the captain's mind were too much to give credence to.

"Look, Tash, I hate to be the one to tell you this, but there's nothing that can 'destroy the world.' When I was a little girl rooting around with the rest of the grounders, before Mama and me learned the Art, we had plenty of Hell-sellers spouting doom-this and doom-that, especially in regards to the Matriarchy. It's all a sham. If you believe you're a harbinger of the end, then you're something I never expected: a fool."

Tash reached down between her legs and rubbed a

finger across her ivory labia. A soft moan of pleasure escaped her lips, and her eyelids fluttered. The automaton's wounds sparked with violet energy in response.

"Uh," Charlotte stumbled, thrown off by the Doll's unexpected actions. "That's not really how arguments are won, Tash. While quite distracting, it doesn't exactly offer a counterpoint to my concerns."

The Doll held up her finger, drawing attention to the glistening moisture on it. Despite being nearly free of the intoxicant now, a deep urge rose in Charlotte to go to the porcelain woman, to lick her fingers, to throw her to the ground and continue down to where the ambrosia was drawn from.

"I see the hunger in your eyes," Tash said, a purr lurking in her voice. "This. This is the doom I speak of."

"What?" Charlotte asked, trying to keep her eyes from traveling back down to between Tash's thighs.

"Focus, please," the Doll said with a hint of impatience. "Imagine, for a moment, that I was set free upon the grounded populace with orders to subdue them. Further, let us postulate that I would be deployed into their halls of power. How long do you think that mankind would last?"

The thought grounded Charlotte's lust like lightning to a rod. A shiver of fear ran through the captain at all the implications. Men had always fought and killed each other over territory, mates, a hundred different reasons, both real and imagined. How would they react to a Doll crafted to be perfect, whose sex was more addictive than opium? Charlotte had lost control when she'd merely had a passing taste, and she was trained in the Art.

Beyond the physical intoxication though was the allure of one of the legendary Doll-demons that men whispered about, their fear mixed with desire at the tales they'd heard. And, although they were no suitable replacement for a tantric practitioner, the Dolls were more proficient than a grounder could imagine in the realm of sexual exploration. Standard models were programmed with a variety of differing techniques to make them an easy source of energy for the engineers. How intricate and detailed would Tash's own knowledge in that realm be? There was no telling how much influence she could wield, and how many people in power would take their countries to war to possess her.

"Now imagine further." Tash whispered, her voice heavy and delicious, tempting Charlotte even though the aviatrix knew to be on guard. "An army of Dolls like myself released upon the world. Whether constructed or born, it is of no consequence, for they will try to replicate whatever I am. This I know."

It was a terrifying idea. Tash had been able to force a trained tantric engineer to obey the Doll's orders, albeit however briefly. Ten, thirty, a hundred of her, more perhaps, could bring untold devastation to the grounders, even if by accident. And if the enhanced Dolls were truly attempting to destroy the nations of the world? Charlotte shuddered to think of the apocalypse that would result. It wasn't just the men who would war over the beautiful automatons; if her reactions to the venom were any indicator the intoxicant Tash produced was just as effective on women as men. Even stodgy old Queen Victoria would hike up her skirts for such a temptress. Failing that, good old human jealousy and fear would send people into just as strong a rage as any lust-fueled technophile.

The *Harlot's Promise* shuddered as one of the flitters fired a shot across the bow, sending ripples through the flight aura. If the enforcers targeted the ship and opened up Charlotte would have no protection. The weaponized tantric beams were impeded by neither flesh nor metal, penetrating physical materials as easily as light through air. Even if they somehow missed the aviatrix, the damage done to the flight aura would be like disrupting a song by screeching off-key, discordant notes that would rob the Liberty Ship of its flight.

The only problem with the tantric stunners was their incredible power needs; enforcers didn't normally travel very far from Godmother for that very reason. But there was no question that Tash was too important to let such considerations stop them. Erin would have no qualms about blowing the drones' entire energy load across the *Harlot's Promise*.

"You must decide my fate, mistress," Tash said, her face going stoic with Charlotte's lengthening silence. "Tarry much longer, and your people will take away the choice."

Rebellious anger sharpened in Charlotte's chest at the mention of "her" people. "Her" people had betrayed her, lied to her, used her. And they wanted to do the same to the Doll, twisting her to a use antithetical to the very philosophical concepts of tantric magic. Instead of freedom, they wanted to bring control and manipulation. It took a jaded and damaged view to think that humanity without an overbearing authority would descend into the depths of primal madness; they ignored the fact that if humans were so inherently awful, they would never have created civilization in the first place.

Fuck "her" people.

"It occurs to me that our pursuers have made a grave mistake," Charlotte said airily, watching the Doll's expression carefully. A glint of hope passed through, and the construct cocked her head quizzically.

"You see," Charlotte continued, "they believe the *Harlot's Promise* to be unarmed, vulnerable. Like any bully, Erin thinks that the ability to impose her will with force means she has power over us."

"Us?" Tash responded, surprise lighting up her face.

Charlotte nodded firmly. "Yes. Us. It's true that the ship doesn't have any way to fight back...but I do. With a bit of luck and a lot of power I can push enough energy out to the flitters to overload their batteries. The enforcers have very basic accumulators; there's no safety to prevent critical failures like larger ships. I'm not sure exactly what will happen, but if luck is on our side the result should be enough to cripple them and let us make our escape."

"That will take an extraordinary amount of magic and control," Tash said doubtfully. "Are you capable of such a feat?"

Charlotte shook her head. "No. But *we* are. From what I've seen you have at least an instinctive amount of control over your abilities. If you lend me a bit of that strength, I think we could do it. The only other alternative is we die."

"No. There is another. You could surrender me to them, mistress," Tash reminded her.

The captain snorted derisively. "Not a chance; I couldn't give you up and live with myself after. You might be a bit delusional, but I can't deny facts staring me in the face. Creating you was a declaration of war against free will itself. There's no way I'm letting the Matriarchy debase itself by doing the same thing to grounders that was done to us for millennia. Men, women, hell, any sentient beings no matter their sexy bits, deserve better. Sure, it'd be easier to hand you over. But it wouldn't be right. Someone's got to stop this authoritarian bullshit they're dead set on shoveling. If not me, then who? If not now, then when?"

Charlotte leaned against the wall and slid down next to Tash. She offered her hand to the automaton.

"Are you ready to help me really piss off the Legion?" the aviatrix asked with a crooked grin.

Tash took Charlotte's proffered hand and pulled her closer, so that their sides and shoulders touched. The Doll then turned Charlotte's palm up, running her fingers across the forearm up to the crook of the aviatrix's elbow and back again. Tash's fingertips were hard, akin to actual nails, and the swiftly-disappearing trace of lighter skin as she stroke-scratched the captain's arm swirled magic playfully through Charlotte's nadi.

"It will take more than holding hands to pull off what you propose," Tash said wickedly.

With gentle firmness the automaton pulled Charlotte so that she sat with back to the Doll. Tash's legs splayed out to either side around her, forming a comfortable triangle that she nestled the captain within. Charlotte was careful to avoid the bullet holes in the automaton's thighs that had finally ceased their sparking bleed of energy. It was likely a trick of her mind, but the aviatrix would have sworn the wounds were smaller and shallower than she remembered. But that was impossible; machines couldn't heal.

Goosebumps prickled along the nape of Charlotte's neck as the lilac-scented breath of the Doll played over it. Tash's hands moved over Charlotte's back, massaging her skin through the scarlet flight leathers. The captain was acutely aware of just how naked the mechanical woman was; Tash's naked breasts pressed into her back as the Doll's hands moved around to the front, bringing with them trails of tantric energy. One hand pressed into the captain's abs, an electrifying feeling through the leather, while the other moved to the aviatrix's thigh, trailing fingers as Tash crept around to the inner thigh. Despite the danger of their pursuers the Doll was taking her time, lighting the fires that Charlotte had tried to keep in check for nearly a month. The teasing proximity of Tash's hands near her most sensitive parts were more arousing than Charlotte had expected. The aviatrix began to grind against the warmth of the Doll, pushing her body closer to the ivory perfection that was fondling her, a hungry whine escaping her lips as her face flushed with excitement.

"You're making it very difficult to remain focused," Charlotte said, her voice unexpectedly husky. A quick check confirmed that no venom from the Doll remained in her system; this was the primitive horniness of a woman who'd been denying herself time with others.

The hairs on Charlotte's arms prickled as Tash gently kissed the back of her neck, moving lips and teeth over to an earlobe.

"I am sorry. Truly," the Doll breathed. "If it makes you feel better, you can punish me later. Mistress."

Charlotte's blood pumped loud in her ears. Snarling in sexual frustration, the captain projected commands through the control ruby, using her unsatisfied craving to craft a suitable answer to the threats behind them.

The flight aura shimmered as the captain pushed her desires through the systems, drawing on the accumulators to supplement her own primal needs. A brilliant spot of amethyst appeared on the invisible aura that surrounded the ship as the condensed energy sought release like a denied lover, pushing, insistent. Charlotte gave into the feeling as Tash's hand moved from the aviatrix's thigh to between her legs, applying pressure as she stroked the captain's sex through her tight pants. The feeling of her cotton panties rubbing against her pussy, barely ghosting past her clit, the smell of leather, and the murmured encouragement from the Doll, all would have been enough to make Charlotte come without the burst of energy that Tash channeled at the height of her excitement.

The *Harlot's Promise* orgasmed as her captain did, a pulsing beam of violet energy flickering into existence between the elegant ship and one of its unmanned pursuers. For a moment, the flitter remained unharmed, the ethereal stream apparently passing through its hull without leaving any visible damage. Then with a crack of thunder the battery at the heart of the enforcer overloaded in an explosion. The shockwave sent the other flitters tumbling away from it. One hit the ocean below with an impact that shattered it like overripe fruit. But the remaining two righted themselves after a moment before zooming after the *Harlot's Promise* once more.

As her mind centered back to her body Charlotte found herself being held firmly by Tash, one arm bracing them with the rail above their head while the other hugged protectively across the aviatrix's chest. The captain was keenly aware of just how warm and soft the automaton's grasp was.

"Thank you," Charlotte croaked, blushing like a virgin at the tenderness of the Doll's warm embrace and panting a bit from the release. Although the aviatrix could see the golden gears and pistons under the translucent skin at the joints between the ivory muscles, her mind screamed that it was a flesh and blood woman holding her.

"An excellent shot, my beautiful captain," Tash murmured in her ear, accompanied by another nibble on her earlobe.

Every nerve Charlotte had was screaming for more, for all of it; the minor orgasm before had merely been the opening salvo of a barrage of insatiable need that was building up every moment. But she fought it off, subsuming her mind in the cold bath of the ship's controls. Charlotte's head cleared, and she was able to extricate herself from the tempting embrace. Tash made tiny, disappointed mewling noises, inflaming the captain's desires. The portion of Charlotte's mind disconnected from the body recognized subliminal mystic encoding within the sounds, the alluring murmur of a lover calling out that people had been embedding inside their entreaties without knowing it since the species began. The Matriarchy had built Tash well for the task of destroying humanity with its own lust. It had never been done with a Doll before, but somehow the engineers that created her had achieved a feat Charlotte had thought was impossible.

Tash was actually using tantric magic.

Whether the Doll knew she was doing it or not was irrelevant. The automaton's skills went far beyond the subconscious magic infusing her sexual venom, and Tash was manipulating it like a skilled engineer, even if by sheer instinct. That a machine, an unliving thing, had been infused with true life and could access a primal sex magic most of the world could not even comprehend...the implications were staggering.

"Enough," Charlotte objected to the Doll's pout. "Tash, you're not helping your case any. If you can't control yourself long enough for us to avoid certain death, then how can I trust anything you're saying?"

The beautiful automaton shook her bald head, visibly stopping herself from yet another overture. When Tash spoke, her voice was tightly controlled.

"My apologies, mistress. It is difficult to think of anything else. Especially when your need is so apparent."

"What about your needs?" Charlotte responded, nodding to the bullet holes in the Doll's legs. The wounds were definitely healing, and rapidly.

"They are one and the same." Even actively suppressing her seduction abilities, Tash still managed to make the half-shrug one of sultry mystery.

"Come again?" Charlotte asked, immediately

regretting it as the Doll smiled mischievously. "Stop that; you know what I meant. How are you healing? At every turn, you blithely reveal another impossibility that you don't even notice in passing."

"I…I am not sure," Tash said, a troubled look crossing her perfect face. "There are many things I both know and do not know. An organic being might consider them instincts. As you have seen, I have yet to master even my own impulses, let alone my memories. I know of you, of the Matriarchy, of many things both seen and unseen. It is all scattered though, like shadows flitting under a frozen lake. I have no idea what monsters swim beneath the surface."

"Let's start with a simple question then: how long have you been active?" Charlotte asked.

"I have been operational for thirty-six minutes."

Charlotte shook her head, vaguely aware through the bond with the *Harlot's Promise* of the enforcer flitters regrouping and stalking the ship. The mountain range ahead was quickly approaching, with nothing but heavy forest below. Whatever small chance of survival a water landing offered was gone now, as banking and heading back out to sea would make them too vulnerable to the flitters. Charlotte knew she should wait until after they'd somehow lost their pursuers to question the Doll, but the mystery of Tash was too much for her inquisitive mind to let rest.

"How in Lilith's name are you this articulate and self-aware? Even the best Doll engineer has to spend a month programming them for their interactions with living people. Even after that their capabilities beyond sexual gratification are limited, at best."

"My first memories are...hazy. Fragmented," Tash said, closing her eyes in concentration. "Confusing. I remember coming into the same room from multiple directions all at once. I see my body from the outside, inert, waiting for...me? Irritation. Elation. Sexual surges beyond description. It's so jumbled. There were people...and then there weren't. Energy, life, all pulsing. Then running, sirens; gunfire. A bullet hitting me is my first clear recollection. A well-muscled redheaded woman shouting. Information, including your rebellious nature and the location of your docking number, flowed into me from there like a waterfall."

"The woman who shot you was Erin. One of the heads of the Legion of Lilith. Also, a massive bitch." Charlotte grimaced. She altered course to try and give them a few more seconds before the flitters caught up. "Better she shot your legs than your heart, at least."

"Pardon?"

"Never mind. It's odd that you have such mental fragmentation. Dolls are perfect from the start; that includes their memories. The only downside is that they are tabula rasa, a blank slate; it takes a while to get them even to where they can walk and talk, let alone what you've demonstrated. You should still be in a sub-verbal state, at best."

"And yet," Tash muttered, gesturing at herself.

"Ignoring reality when it doesn't match up with what you expect is the hallmark of the stupid," Charlotte agreed. "Listen, if we can get clear, we'll sort this out. But first—"

The *Harlot's Promise* shuddered as the last two flitters

caught up and opened fire. The internal speakers stayed silent save for static, and only by rotating the frequency of the flight aura was Captain Frost able to keep them flying.

The flitters were done with warnings.

"Perhaps you should hand me over, mistress," Tash said with measured calmness. "Without clear recollection, I may indeed be the murderer that your redhead claimed."

"Not mine," Charlotte corrected her, a little too quickly.

"Regardless," the Doll pressed on. "I may be a lethal entity. For your safety, you should turn me over. In the heat of the moment, out of desperation, I endangered you, an action I now regret. Far better that I had plunged to my death alone than to drag you down with me."

Charlotte banked the ship hard to avoid the lance shots from the flitters, buying them some breathing room. It was a lucky dodge; even if she managed to evade a few beams, eventually the flitters would widen their weapons spread to bathe the ship in energy. The method would take longer to bring down the Liberty Ship's flight aura, but it was a sure thing against most aviatrixes. And although Lauren had been one of those ace pilots that could outfly even those shots, Charlotte's talents lay elsewhere. She was, at her heart, an engineer. The mantle of captain was an uncomfortable one.

"That's not really your call though, is it?" Charlotte responded to Tash, her mind more on the serpentine pattern she was trying to weave to avoid the blasts. "You don't get to decide whether I put myself in the way of the bully and their victim. We all roll our dice and take our chances. What you're willing to bet and why is the measure of your character."

"I am a weapon. That much is clear," Tash replied, a tinge of resentment toward herself threading the words.

"Have you harmed anyone since your mind cleared and became able to process thought and action?" Charlotte asked. Another volley of energy was met with another hard bank of the ship. The angle of the tilt was enough to slide Charlotte back into Tash's grasp. Although the flight aura compensated for inertia to a certain extent, it was being hard pressed by their evasive maneuvers. The *Harlot's Promise* groaned as the ship's hull struggled to hold together under Charlotte's piloting.

"I threatened you with it," Tash replied bitterly. "Enslavement of a sentient for my own freedom. Inexcusable. The reasoning I gave myself was that survival demanded it; but was I just as mercenary before? Did I feel my life was in danger, that self-preservation superseded the lives of others? What if in my fragmentary memory state, I did murder someone?"

Charlotte dove the ship to avoid a volley of energy from the pursuing flitters; Tash encircled her with one slender arm, using the other to help brace them both on the carpeted floor.

"Can we maybe discuss this later?" the aviatrix asked. The Doll's embrace was both reassuring and distracting. "We've got bigger problems now."

"Not if you hand me over," Tash answered, her voice quavering with false bravado.

"Enough of that," Charlotte said, pulling her

concentration out of the ship's systems enough to lock the golden gaze of the Doll. "I said what I said, and that's that. Your very existence begs the question: what were you built for if not a subtle war? There's no surfeit of feminine sexual energy available on tap in Godmother. Beyond that, why go to all the time and trouble to construct a Doll that's actually alive? More to the point: how? You are a work of art that I did not believe was possible. That should not be possible. An artificial soul, a mind that reasons and has desires? That is beyond anything I ever imagined.

"Besides," the aviatrix said with a smirk, "It'll really piss off Erin."

Charlotte Frost's rebellious grin froze into a rictus as the flitters widened their tantric beams, bathing the ship and the cabin in amethyst energy.

Chapter 4

The world went hazy for Charlotte, becoming a painter's mix of colors and form. Solid outlines melded with each other, as if the very universe were merely a masterpiece left out in the storm. The colors clung to each other, caressing, comforting, all the world together in the downpour of life. Her mind partially subsumed in the *Harlot's Promise*, Charlotte's own response was amplified even more by the sizzling power as the flitters bathed both the Liberty Ship and its mistress in augmented tantric energy. Science and magic intermixed into a potent brew that was unlike anything any aviatrix had ever experienced before.

"That is…invigorating…" Tash said at the edge of the captain's consciousness, her tone thick with stimulation. "I am finding it difficult to…keep my thoughts from… mistress? You do not look well…"

The touch of the magnificent Doll on Charlotte's skin was lightning, an electricity far beyond anything Faraday or Ohm ever dreamt of. All the resistance to her urges the aviatrix had been holding on to evaporated, replaced with an overwhelming hunger, a lust.

A need.

Charlotte spun in Tash's lap, hooking her legs over and grabbing onto Tash like a lioness with its prey. Fingers, mouth, body, the aviatrix hungrily pressed herself against every available inch. The Doll's eyes widened in joyful surprise, her own desire rising to the occasion.

"Captain Frost," Tash breathed heavily as Charlotte roughly grabbed one of the Doll's voluptuous breasts, her tongue encircling the golden nipple as she sucked at it.

Her other hand snaked its way down the taut ivory belly until her fingers found the Doll's wet and willing pussy. Despite her savage needs, the aviatrix's attunement to tantric magic guided her fingers into a gentle firmness as Charlotte teased the soft ivory hood of the Doll's pussy, using her thumb to pull it back ever so slightly so that the clit was fully exposed. Tiny jolts of tantric energy stimulated it as Charlotte used both her physical and mystical skills to make Tash release a deep moan.

"Mistress," Tash tried again, fighting to hold onto rational thought as the violet energy bathing the ship reflected off the windows, creating a rainbow kaleidoscope within the cabin. "Please. Are you sure you want this?"

In answer Charlotte slid her middle two fingers up into Tash, penetrating the willing Doll with a growl of possessiveness. Both women, one of ivory and one of flesh, felt their minds melting into each other, the natural resonance of desire amplified a hundredfold by the tantric energy weapons of their pursuers. Seeking fingers pressed further into the welcoming heat; tremors of pleasure shot through Tash. Charlotte gave no thought to the ship, no worry about the faltering flight aura. Nothing else mattered other than her lust, and in her primality, she craved Tash to join her in the coming apocalypse. A few inches of gentle but insistent probing by the captain's fingers found the spot she was looking for.

Tash discovered with a gasp that her clit was not alone in being an erogenous zone. As soon as Charlotte felt the differing texture of the spot, she gave the Doll a wicked smile and began to move her fingers back and forth, faster and faster, teasing and taunting the extra-sensitive area as she made her fingers tingle with tantric energy.

"Come for me," Charlotte demanded, moving up Tash's chest to her neck then face, nibbling the pale cheek with her teeth. "Fucking come for me! You are mine!"

Tash felt heat she didn't expect, emanating not just from her sex but also from her mechanical heart, a quake of forbidden and longed-for sin that pulsed in time with the tantric energy bathing the ship in increasing amounts. Something shifted in the Doll, a massive shadow moving under the ice sheet covering her memory. A hidden protocol engaged, a chamber in her mind opening its secret doors to accept Charlotte's presence just as her pussy had accepted the captain's fingers.

"Say it!" Charlotte roared, her mind addled beyond reason by now, her lust uncontained by the mental link she still shared with the ship. "Tell me. Tell me you're mine. Say it!"

Tash exploded with a scream of pure bliss. "Yes! I am yours, my captain, my mistress, my everything! Take it all!"

A fresh burst of amethyst magic filled the cabin at the

moment of the Doll's orgasm, taking Tash beyond logic and reason and threatening a mystic overload to both of their minds. Charlotte lost all semblance of control, pulling her fingers out of the twitching Doll and taking hold of her head firmly with both hands.

Charlotte pulled Tash into a long and passionate kiss, their tongues darting and intertwining as their lips moved on each other, energy coursing between them as the captain siphoned the excess magic off her lover. Their minds swirled together in an ecstatic state that Charlotte had never experienced. The aviatrix broke the kiss first, her hands moving up to the back of Tash's head and pressing down with a savage insistence.

Tash smiled mischievously as she obeyed the needs of her captain. She kissed and nibbled on her way down Charlotte's face to her neck, unbuttoning the top of the dark red flight leathers and yanking them open. Charlotte's small but full breasts stood pert and ready for the Doll's attention, and the captain hissed in anticipation as Tash ran her hands across them gently, pinching the erect nipples slightly before licking them teasingly. Charlotte mewled in need, and Tash enveloped the aureole with her lips, sucking and tugging on them each in turn as she caressed the other. More pressure on the top of her head though told the Doll that her mistress required more.

The ivory automaton licked and kissed her way down to the top of the pants, looking up at Charlotte with golden eyes. When the aviatrix looked down Tash locked gazes with her as she used her teeth and tongue to work open the buttons of the leather trousers. Charlotte's eyes were wide and crazed with lust, and she writhed under the Doll's slow tease before Tash yanked the captain's pants off with a single savage motion. Charlotte's boots came tumbling off with it, and Charlotte's naked body pressed against every inch of Tash that she could. Already out of their minds with wanton lust, their shared desires were infused again by another blast from the pursuing enforcers.

Charlotte bolted to her feet, bracing one foot on the railing and opening herself at head-level to the Doll, her pussy wet with heady excitement. The aviatrix's hands pressed against the back of Tash's head as a growl of need escaped her throat.

"Eat my pussy, damn it!" the captain scream-ordered with a begging edge.

The Doll rose to her knees, ignoring the leg wounds as they fully healed up from the tantric energy saturating the cabin. She grabbed Charlotte's toned buttocks with both hands and pulled her loins in.

Tash's tongue was firm and certain as she went to work on the captain's pussy. Licking, nibbling, using her lips to lightly suck on the clit and repaying Charlotte's fingering with tonguework that found the captain's most sensitive spots. The captain screamed in pleasure and lost what little grip on reality she had under Tash's focused attentions.

The violet light filling the ship now came not from any weaponry being fired, but rather, radiated from the aviatrix being eaten out by the Doll. Tash was tireless, as were her tongue and lips, and her tactics changed as the automaton subconsciously took notes of what her mistress enjoyed most among the varied techniques. The sex-generated violet light pulsed with every orgasm, the magic growing stronger as Charlotte's own reactions did. Under the carpeted floor the accumulators of the ship responded to its captain's joy, pulsing with raw tantric energy.

Gravity tilted as the flight aura sputtered and failed.

Tash had trouble concentrating on anything other than pleasuring her mistress, digging her fingertips into Charlotte's ass cheeks, timing her tongue strokes with the scratches she was leaving in a song of pleasure and pain that made the aviatrix come harder and harder.

At the edge of her mind the Doll recognized they were in danger, that their embrace would end in a fiery demise for both. Captain Frost's mental connection to the ship couldn't overcome the constant mystical attacks from the pursuing flitters. The strange protocol in Tash's mind that had locked in on Charlotte by the intense sex within the bath of mystic energy overrode a section of her lust, granting a sliver of control now that her mistress's life was in danger.

Energized by the enforcers' constant barrage of magic, a supercharged Tash sent her mind out through the ephemeral network, using her physical and emotional connection with Charlotte to seek the captain's scattered will along the lines of sexual force running through the ship, all without stopping her oral pleasuring of the captain. It felt to Tash as if she had gone beyond merely supping on Charlotte's sex to pleasuring the aviatrix's soul.

Like a ghost ranting to itself, the two minds found each other in the pulsing primal dream of the tantric state, their mingled souls burning with brilliance. A hybrid overmind rose above the maelstrom of desire, and the flight aura sprang back into existence around the *Harlot's Promise*, leveling off the ship before it crashed into the earth below. The ship became as much an extension of their existences as each other, and as the captain suddenly started orgasming the hull screamed in joy with a spurt of speed, unconsciously angling the ship up as they reached the coastal mountain range. Treetops whizzing by scant feet away from the hull were like Tash's tongue, teasing, pleasing, mouth firm and hungry on Charlotte's pussy.

The enforcer flitters strained to keep up as the Liberty Ship shot away up the wooded slope. Annoyed by the buzzing of the mechanical insects pursuing them, the combined creature of Charlotte, Tash, and the *Harlot's Promise* turned its attention back to the pitiful things. The hybrid's world was energy and pulses of fleshy pleasure within its hull, and the trailing craft possessed naught but hollow echoes of joy and pleasure trapped in the batteries at their unfeeling cores. The Liberty Ship's flight aura frequency was changing rapidly in time to her captain's orgasms, making it effectively immune to the disruptive effects of the enforcers' tantric lances.

Left with no other option to stop them, the flitters streaked forward, their power cores pushed to the limit as Godmother piloted them on a suicide course for the *Harlot's Promise*.

Locked together in the hybrid overmind, Tash and Charlotte opened their mouths in unison and keened an unearthly harmony.

A tantric shockwave pulsed from the *Harlot's Promise* in a cone back at the enforcers, charged with more sexual energy than any battery could contain. The flitters suffered premature detonation as their cores overloaded from the influx of raw power, exploding harmlessly in the air before they were close enough to scratch the immaculate hull of the *Harlot's Promise*. Their wreckage left a fiery path as their remains plowed into the wooded slope, but the forest was heavy with moisture, limiting the spread of the flames.

The shockwave of energy was as if the Liberty Ship itself had orgasmed, drawing off massive amounts of magic from its batteries and releasing Charlotte and Tash from the clutches of the hybrid overmind they'd become. The *Harlot's Promise* crested the mountain range rapidly, leveling out for a moment before her nose dipped to follow the slope down toward the arid terrain on the other side.

Charlotte and Tash slumped away from each other on the carpeted floor, exhausted, and the ship's flight aura sputtered dangerously, the drained batteries struggling to keep them aloft. Captain Frost was able to level the ship off as they left the coastal mountain range behind, the terrain rapidly moving from scrubland to rocky desert.

The *Harlot's Promise* came in hard, but Charlotte maintained enough control to keep the rough landing from doing any real damage, reversing the pontoon engines to try and brake. Great gouts of sand spewed from the front of the ship like ocean waves as the Liberty Ship plowed into the ground, its hull held together by libidium and luck. They plowed a furrow in the desert as the airship bled off its speed, finally coming to rest with a groan as it listed to the side in the blazing sun like an animal in its death throes.

Tash held tight to Charlotte once more, keeping her from breaking her neck in the controlled crash.

The tantric flying aura flickered at the edge of awareness before fading with a pop and crackle that was less than encouraging.

Tash released the captain, smiling with tenderness at how sweaty the aviatrix had become from their sexual escapades. Charlotte gave a relieved huff, her top pulled open with breasts glistening. From waist down she was naked, and the carpet felt comforting on her bare bottom.

"I need pants."

Tash snorted a giggle, but her mirth was dampened as Charlotte rolled over to face her with a mixed expression of guilt and desire.

"I want to…" Charlotte started, stumbling over the words, her eyes lingering on the Doll's hairless sex, still pristine and tempting.

"Shhh, no, my dear captain," Tash shushed with a purr, placing a silencing forefinger over Charlotte's lips. "I know. You wish to reciprocate, but the venom of my love is too dangerous to taste again. I understand. But you need not worry about my pleasures. In addition to your excellent fingerwork, I was able to sample your orgasms sufficiently."

Tash drew Charlotte's hand down to her bare leg. Where before there had been a bullet hole, there was now naught but smooth ivory skin. The aviatrix knew how to alter the flows in her own body and others to accelerate natural regenerative processes, but a Doll was nothing more than a golem, a construct that required work by sweat and hammers to make whole.

"You repaired yourself. That should be impossible," Charlotte said in amazement.

"Healed," Tash corrected. "I healed myself. I am no simple pocket watch, mistress. As you should well know by now."

The aviatrix gave her a crooked grin. "Fair enough."

Charlotte hauled herself to her feet, as did Tash.

"Well," the captain sighed heavily. "Let's see how bad it is."

The anteroom they'd been inhabiting was small, but its door led directly to the largest section of the quarterdeck. Shadows played along the walls as they entered, the dusk outside the windows barely providing any light, so Charlotte waved her hand across a panel and channeled a tiny amount of energy. Quartz crystals across the Harlot's Promise blazed to life, a simple and effective light system that dispelled the gloom.

The lion's share of the quarterdeck was given over to the needs of the refugees the Liberty Ship's transported. Twenty beds with sheets were bolted firmly to the floor, their underside given over to drawers and storage space that wouldn't budge even in the worst of turbulence or piloting. They were arrayed next to the windows for a spectacular view designed to give hope and awe to any who needed it. But there was also a series of curtains that could be drawn for those who didn't care for heights or the outside world. Lighter curtains could be pulled to give a measure of privacy to each bunk, even if only in a tiny space. The center of the quarterdeck was a massive clothes rack, carrying hundreds of outfits in a staggering array of sizes and styles. In addition to providing for the needs of those who'd fled abusive lives with nothing to their names, the collection of attire was handy for when an aviatrix wanted to blend in more easily among the various cultures and nations that they were wont to visit in their missions. Small strips of cloth hooked into a floor-mounted rail, helping to keep the clothes rack as secured as the furniture in transit. Beyond the refugee quarters there was a section usually given over to crew members, but since converted to extra space for passengers by the Frost wives. To the fore and aft of the deck there were stairways up and down, as well as various storage cabinets.

"You should avail yourself of some of those," Charlotte said, motioning to the massive clothes rack.

"What, you do not wish me to continue prancing around in the nude?" Tash asked mischievously, posing in a faux-innocent way that sent Charlotte's imagination into a spiral.

"I need to be able to concentrate on my ship's body, not yours," Charlotte laughed. "You're far too distracting for me to get any work done like that."

Tash bit her lip in a show of bratty petulance while batting her eyes innocently before breaking into a giggle. "As you say, my captain. Besides, what seduction would be complete without gift-wrapping the present first? We have gone a bit in reverse, I would say, putting the main course before the appetizer."

Charlotte chortled as she left the beautiful automaton to sort through the clothes and choose an outfit. The captain took the back stairs down to the engineering deck, running her hands over the interior hull as she sought breaks in the material. Although strained to its limit, the *Harlot's Promise* was a tough ship, and she'd taken the rough landing without any apparent hull damage beyond paint scrapes.

A quick check of the accumulator system and the ship's internal wiring confirmed Charlotte's suspicions: drained. There was enough residual energy for lights, and that was about it. Although their lovemaking had helped to direct and power the massive wave of magic that had detonated the enforcers, the expenditure had used up their fuel reserves. Fortunately, the flight aura's mechanical components were otherwise undamaged. But without charged batteries, the airship was as dead in the sand as any other boat dropped in the middle of the desert. And just as vulnerable.

Charlotte headed for the top deck as fast as she could, using the stairs to work out some of her irritation. She came to the door to the captain's quarters and fought against the pit in her stomach as she unlatched it and stepped inside.

The captain's quarters were spacious, with charts and navigational apparatus covering the closed shelves. Charlotte gave the private cabin only a cursory glance before continuing through to the open air of the top deck. She hadn't set foot inside the cabin since the split with Lauren, instead sleeping in the refugee quarters, and then only infrequently. She'd been avoiding laying down as much as possible, staying busy with the maintenance that every Liberty Ship demanded. Every time she laid down Charlotte could only remember Lauren, remember resting her head on the other woman's chest as they slept. That soothing rhythm of breathing in and out of her wife had been a comforting warmth that lulled Charlotte to sleep many nights. Without it, she felt lost. The bed was a lonely and cold place to the betrayed.

Night was coming on fast, and despite the heat of the day the gritty desert wind had the bite of cold to it now. Although she was exhausted, Charlotte felt urgent and restless. They'd managed to escape the enforcer flitters, but it wouldn't take much work for another Liberty Ship to retrace their course and find the Harlot's Promise. The desert offered precious little concealment beyond the occasional scraggly tree and spindly bush, and the grounded craft could be easily seen by anyone within several miles. The need to get airborne again and out of harm's way was almost palatable. Charlotte didn't know where they'd go, where'd they hide from the Matriarchy. But in the middle of the Syrian Desert was the worst place to try.

"The damage does not appear to be severe," Tash opined from the stairwell at the end of the deck.

Charlotte felt flushed as the newly-dressed Doll emerged from the shadows. Tash had chosen a frayed peasant's dress and bustier, trying to dress down as much as she could at her captain's request. But the curves of her body and the sensual way she moved would have rendered a potato sack as sexy as lingerie. The Doll had even gone to the trouble of choosing a simple bonnet to wear over her bald head with a light veil. Charlotte nodded approvingly; although there was no hiding what Tash was close up, from a distance she'd appear as any other buxom woman.

"You're right," Charlotte replied, swaying a little with how tired she was. "But that's not the problem."

"Mistress?" Tash said with worry, quickly moving to support the fatigued captain.

"Even if you hadn't given me a good tongue-lashing, it took a bit out of me to focus our energy into destroying the enforcers," Charlotte said. "Unfortunately, it also drained the batteries. We don't have enough juice to get airborne again, or even to maintain a flight aura or run the pontoon props if we did."

"Oh?" Tash said with a naughty tone. "I will happily volunteer to help you generate more tantric energy. For the batteries, of course. All very professional."

Charlotte let out a short laugh but worry nibbled at the edge of it. "It's not that simple, my hungry little Doll. There's a different frequency, a unique flavor, that goes with every kind of sex and sexuality. It modulates based on the person, on the form of activity, gender identity, and a thousand other tiny details unique to each soul. The blast we let loose earlier drained the male-aspected energy from the ship's stores. While I'm sure you'd have no trouble helping me create enough sapphic magic to support that side of the equation, without the masculine we're still not going anywhere."

"So, we need a man?" Tash said, cocking her head quizzically.

"To put it simply: yes," Charlotte shrugged. "A male who'd find me attractive, specifically."

Tash snorted in feigned disbelief, but the captain waved her off.

"I'm serious. A man who only desires other men generates a particular wavelength of energy, as does a woman who only desires women. The reaction we need to reinvigorate our accumulators can only be generated by the two sides of the coin. It's the rarest of energy resources on Godmother, given their isolationist policies. There are aviatrixes that tend toward the male portion of the spectrum, some even straddling the line or fully embracing it and able to generate the same energy. But they're shunned for their feelings, made to feel uncomfortable, shuffled off to the surface in the name of so-called 'real' men and women. Short-sighted and idiotic. The ideals of the Matriarchy have become tainted by the very exclusion that they decry in the men. We make outcasts of the outcast and are no better for it as a result."

The Doll shook her head in wonderment. "Even though they lack the equipment, those who show the mannerisms of the hated sex are not tolerated? That seems rather foolish for a mystical system based on such close relationships."

Captain Frost laughed bitterly. "Tolerance. It's a funny thing. For centuries, for millennia, women have borne the brunt of the mistakes of man, the pain and envy of them, right alongside gay folk, people of color, and anything else not starchy white in both appearance and mannerisms. When given a taste of power that is theirs alone, any group that's been stepped on for centuries is going to bite the foot through the boot. The problem is knowing when to stop, when you go from being a liberator to an oppressor. It chafes my tits that the Matriarchy doesn't know or care if other forms of magic and thought have become viable. No one understands why ancient tantric techniques and knowledge suddenly became feasible, powerful. Hell, we haven't even figured out the Bright Barrier that cut the western hemisphere off from the rest of the world when the mystic forces flooded reality. Is anyone even still alive there? Were they responsible, or are they victims? Half the world can't be reached anymore, and everyone, including the Matriarchy, lost exploration teams that tried. After a while it just seemed like no one cared how or why the world changed so fundamentally. A century ago, people using sex 'magic' couldn't light a candle with an orgy. These days..."

Vaguely gesturing at Tash and her existence, the meaning was clear to the Doll. In a span of a few decades magic had gone from superstitious fantasy to a reality that not only matched normal technology but superseded it, consuming the Americas in a blinding light that no one ever returned from.

"Are those in power incapable of tantric practices, then?" Tash asked.

"Men?" Charlotte snorted. "There's no reason that they couldn't, with proper training, humility, and empathy. It's those last two stipulations that get in their way though. Pride and arrogance are the natural enemies of knowledge. And the Matriarchy simply doesn't trust any man to be taught our ways, even were he willing and able to learn them."

"Can not the Matriarchy be made to see reason?"

"Talk and walk," Charlotte said, moving past Tash and back down the stairs. The Doll stayed close as they descended into the battery hold.

"Ignorance and pride cuts both ways, Charlotte continued. "There's good and there's bad aboard Godmother, just like the rest of the world. Yeah, we could extend a handout to others just as stepped-on, try and share our mystical techniques with the oppressed. But humanity has never been particularly good at giving power to the best of us, and nothing about tantric magic inherently makes us better people for using it. Sure, you need compassion and can't be a lunatic to practice the Art, but as the stunners that brought us down prove even the most benign concepts can be turned to violence if an asshole tries hard enough. Once you get comfortable being on top, justifications to stay there flow as fast and free as a waterfall."

The dark banks of the eight giant batteries that powered the *Harlot's Promise* swallowed Charlotte as she continued to rage against the inequities of the world and the Matriarchy's failure to share their knowledge with the world. Even in the gloom of the hold the batteries glittered with the embedded accumulator crystals, able to absorb mystic fuel from any sexual activities onboard. Tash could only follow about half of Charlotte's rant as her captain ducked in and out of the darkness, working with wrench and hammer to try and draw a spark of magic from the drained machines. But no amount of cursing or raging could pull blood from a stone. There was no energy to be had, and no matter how much sex they had it would be insufficient to supply the missing frequency.

Tash felt a new emotion: frustration. The desire to help her captain was a physical need, an impulse as strong as hunger or breath. Somewhere within her the Doll could sense the answer lurking, the knowledge like a word on the tip of the tongue, maddening in how close it was.

The need to be useful to Captain Frost was overloading Tash's senses. There'd been a shift in her core when they were bathed in the weaponized tantric energies, a switch thrown that she could neither explain nor reverse. The protocols and hidden directives that comprised her unconscious mind, the essence of what she was, had been altered by the overload of tantric magic she's experienced with Charlotte during the attack. Tash knew it as certainly as she knew that water was wet and fire was hot, a primitive and unchangeable fact. It was as if a massive earthquake had happened deep within her, too far down to show immediately on the surface, but sufficient and long-lasting enough to move continents.

Charlotte Frost was now the center of Tash's universe, every thought and action evaluated in relation to how it would affect her mistress.

Where before the Doll could only think of escape, now she found it difficult to imagine a future where she was not at the aviatrix's side. Knowing that she could help Charlotte if she could just remember how was like grit in her gears, tearing Tash up from the inside out. It was a physical pain enflaming her soul, a wave of terrifying heat that…

"Oh, my," Tash said softly.

The burning need to help Charlotte, the heat radiating from her overwhelming imperative was not in her imagination.

The Doll felt fire spreading through her body.

"Um, mistress?" Tash tried to say. But her jaw clenched, the words refused to come out clearly. They were too deep, too sharp, jumbled. Her limbs began to jerk of their own accord.

Tash collapsed on the hardwood floor of the hold, spasming uncontrollably as her hands began ripping off the peasant's dress of their own accord. The world was too hot, too painful.

The clockwork courtesan panicked, unable to call out to her captain for help, the mechanical seizures screeching in her veins as if terrified rats were clawing their way out. Tash looked down in horror while her pale skin rippled like water. Her arms and legs became heavier, the mass of her large ivory breasts collapsing into her chest. Artificial muscles bulged heavier from redistributed mass, hips cracking as they narrowed, buttocks hardening as they tightened and became more chiseled.

Tash's hands became thicker and heavier as she ran them over her body in frantic confusion. Her skin roughened, chest widening and firming up like melted wax cooling in the snow as the synthetic flesh settled. New sensations overwhelmed the pain, and as the burning receded into the background the Doll cried out in surprise.

"Captain?" Tash shouted in alarm. The automaton's voice boomed strong and heavy through the hold of the ship, startling her with its bass. "Captain Frost! Charlotte! I need you!"

Irritated sounds came from the battery stacks as the aviatrix extricated herself from the accumulator that she'd been pulling apart in the vain hope of discovering any lurking ergs of power. Charlotte yanked the goggles off her eyes with a growl, her attention still focused on the stubborn machinery behind her.

"What, what?" Charlotte said, trying her best not to yell at the Doll. "I've got work to do if we're going to…oh… um…what in the name of Lilith?"

Charlotte's shocked expression confirmed to Tash that she wasn't suffering some form of mechanical delusion.

"Not to alarm you, Captain Frost," the Doll said in her new, deeper voice. "But I may be able to offer a solution to our current predicament."

Charlotte laughed incredulously, doubting her own sanity.

"Tash…is that…did you…did you grow a *dick*?"

Chapter 5

The thick cock-shaped outline that stretched the cotton underpants to their limits was undeniable.

Charlotte gave a low whistle of appreciation at the bulge. The dress that Tash had been wearing was shredded by the automaton's change, leaving only the too-tight underwear holding back the very real flaccid penis. The rest of the Doll's body had also changed into a new masculine form, a porcelain version of da Vinci's Vitruvian Man in all its idealized perfection. Tash had grown by at least six inches in height, with wide shoulders and leanly muscled arms and thighs. Although still bald, the Doll's face had also changed, sharpening in its lines with a longer and more pronounced chin. With her trained engineer's eyes Charlotte noted that the apparent extra mass was simply a redistribution of the automaton's parts. Thinking of her sore shoulder, she realized why she hadn't been prepared for just how heavy Tash had been; the Doll's innards had been densely packed, allowing the transformation from Aphrodite to Adonis.

"Captain? What has happened to me?" Tash pleaded.

There was a desperation, a terror in the automaton's eyes that made Charlotte want to reach out and hold the Doll. Mechanical or not, Tash was a sentient being in pain, and the natural instincts of humanity softened Charlotte's reaction.

"I...I don't know, Tash," the captain said gently. "But you appear to have changed physical sex."

"No, no, that is not correct..." Tash mumbled.

Charlotte pulled her aetheric goggles up to her eyes. Her breath caught in her throat when she looked at the Doll. When Tash had first boarded the airship, the Doll had possessed the aura of the feminine, a strong and powerful frequency that had been undeniably that of a living woman. But the wavelength the goggles were showing Charlotte were of a different hue now, a darker gold and silver.

Tash was now broadcasting the unmistakable aura of a man.

"I'm sorry, Tash, I don't know why, but the readings are irrefutable. Surely you must feel the change in your emotional subroutines as well?"

Tash shook their head. "Captain Frost, you misunderstand. What I meant was that my name is no longer Tash."

Charlotte cocked her head quizzically. "How do you mean?"

"My name is Arslan," the Doll said, his voice firming up as had his body. He stretched as if just awaken, making the sculpted silver-lined musculature contrast with the golden cogs and gears at his joints. He held up a hand, flexing it in wonderment before dropping it to absent-mindedly brush against the outline of his prodigious dick. "And, yes, I am very male."

Charlotte took a step backward, confusion furrowing her brows.

"Okay…but your aura is that of Tash's, if only tuned to a different frequency. Had whatever change you gone through wiped your memory? Is this why you don't recall earlier than boarding my ship?"

"No, nothing like that," Arslan said, a trace of annoyance creeping into his voice. The tiny gears and ivory muscles of his face were just as realistically human as Tash's had been. "I can feel her. Feel me. Still within. But I am Arslan. She is Tash. I am Arslan Tash."

"I am truly confused," Charlotte said with a helpless shrug. "Don't mistake me, I'm more than familiar with the transition from aviatrix to aviator and back again. Some tantric engineers sculpt their flesh to follow their soul, others stay their hand and pursue life as born, and everything in between. Regardless, it really doesn't matter whether the body is altered or not; a soul doesn't change its truth. In a world of subjectivity, the divine spark is a fixed point in the universe, an objective fact that nothing can alter. It's the closest thing to a god that we've ever been able to perceive."

"Your philosophy is sound, I will grant you," Arslan said, nodding as his hands ran across his body appreciatively. Charlotte's eyes kept being drawn back to the Doll's barely contained manhood. If it were anything like Tash's vagina, it'd be a master sculptor's vision of the perfect penis, although at a larger size than ancient artists would have been comfortable with. It would have been less lewd to let it hang free than push against the tight underclothes, which invited stares of appreciation. "But I can only tell you what is, not what should be. I am currently Arslan. I have been Tash. There exist not two minds, but rather, offshoots of the same."

"Wait a minute," Charlotte said. "Tash never mentioned her other side, or mind-sibling, or whatever you think of yourself as. Are there any more of you hiding in there?"

The Doll palmed his face in a too-human expression of frustration. "She, I, did not know about he, him…me! Now that I have transformed, the ice shattered from this persona, allowing transition. Tash will remember my thoughts as I remember hers. But I do believe that despite our confusion that there are only two complete entities inhabiting this body."

"Are you saying you can return to your female form?" Charlotte asked, a bit too quickly. Her recent lovemaking with the Doll were still fresh in the captain's mind, and there was a sense of loss at the thought of not seeing Tash again that she had not expected.

"Why would it be otherwise?" Arslan asked in confusion.

"Why is the sky blue, or blood red?" Charlotte sighed.

"The sky has a hue resultant from the scattering of sunlight as it impacts atmospheric molecules," Arslan said, as if in recitation of a lecture. "Hemoglobin is the active oxygen-carrier in humans and is iron rich, resulting in a…

why are you looking at me like that? Ah. Were you being facetious in your questions?"

"I'm not an idiot," Charlotte said through clenched teeth. "I understand basic science. What I meant is that you are so unknown, it might well be some primal law of the universe that you change irreversibly into a male because of some obscure priming sequence."

"Captain, I am sorry, but I must again correct you," Arslan replied, raising his hands in defense at the irritated look Charlotte gave him. "The reason for the activation of Arslan, of me, is quite apparent.

"It was you."

The accusation fueled Charlotte's rising temper.

"Care to run that one by me again, for your own self-preservation?" the captain growled, pulling the goggles off so she could stare Arslan down properly.

"That is not what I meant to imply!" Arslan said hurriedly. "Quite the opposite, actually. I bear the same directives and emotions about you as Tash. We are bonded to you. But she was not what you needed at that moment. I was. I *am*. So, I shifted accordingly to serve you."

The earnest way he said it, the pleading in his eyes; Charlotte believed Arslan. As her smoldering anger cooled off, the aviatrix's curiosity reasserted itself.

"But your *soul*. The basis of all life. It's changed, and that's just impossible."

Arslan shrugged and gestured at himself. "And, yet, it did. Your failure to adequately define my existence does not negate it. No amount of denial can change reality."

Charlotte pinched her eyes and fought to stay calm.

"Fair enough. But your ability to alter your soul's frequency, its gender, that is just unheard of."

"Not anymore," Arslan said simply.

The aviatrix grappled with the disproval of one of the fundamental tenets of tantric engineering. In transferring the mystic energies to materials and devices, there were immutable laws, just as in science. There was one right way, and a hell of a lot of wrong ones. That somehow Tash had become annoying in the transition, that was the sticking point that had barbed the realization that perhaps their understanding of the Art was not as complete as they'd thought. What else could Tash, no, Arslan Tash, reveal to...

"That's where I know it from!" Charlotte suddenly cried out, snapping her fingers in excitement.

Arslan jumped, startled at the captain's proclamation.

"Captain, what do you— "

"This way!" Charlotte cut him off, grabbing the automaton's hand and pulling him across the foredeck toward the captain's cabin in the rear.

"As you wish, my captain!" the Doll said with a wicked grin, reaching down to tear his smallclothes off and releasing his cock.

Charlotte's reply was cut off as she saw a sculptor's vision of penile perfection freed from its constraints.

As a professional partaker of sex, the aviatrix had seen many versions of penises and vaginas over the years, including those who displayed qualities of both and sometimes of neither. Human sexual biology was as unique and varied as the species itself, but they all had their appeal.

Still, when Charlotte thought of a man or woman, she inevitably had a mental picture of what she was referring to. Plato would have called it the Form of the object, the idealized version from which all others sprang.

Someone had taken that artistic concept and sculpted it into a penis.

Arslan's dick was pale and strong, laying flaccid over a pair of testicles, an extra feature most Dolls were built without. Normal automatons were never so detailed, and the inclusion of a feature largely viewed as superfluous to aviatrix pleasure puzzled the captain. The sheathe for Arslan's cock was smooth and flawless, with tiny veins of gold shining through the skin in places. The head of the shaft peeked out from the foreskin as if it were shy; an evil little voice told Charlotte that it was not. The thickness promised a fulfilling experience rather than a painful one; compared to the simple jackhammer of the Dolls Erin had designed, it was as comparing the touch of silk to rusted iron. The captain could almost feel the heat of the shaft in her hand as she imagined pulling back the foreskin to reveal the perfect cock in all its glory.

"Captain?" Arslan asked, concerned by their slowing pace as Charlotte fought back fantasies of mounting him right there. The battery stacks on the engineering deck would be a far better place for festivities.

"Hmm?" the aviatrix said, realizing she'd been sucking on her lower lip. "Oh, nothing, nothing. I'll, uh, tell you later."

The Doll's smile returned, although there was a strange hesitancy to it, almost a shyness.

As Charlotte led him into the captain's quarters, she ignored the door that led to the spacious bedroom at the back of the ship, instead turning to a wall filled with rolled-up maps on shelves, muttering to herself as she released the Doll's hand. Charlotte went from alcove to alcove, examining each map's hand-lettered labels until she gave a cry of excitement and pulled one from the assortment.

"I knew your name sounded familiar," Charlotte crowed victoriously, spreading out the rolled-up map over the ornate navigator table bolted to the center of the front room. She pulled small inset clamps out from the edge of the table and pinned the map in place with a practiced ease.

"Here. Look right here," the aviatrix ordered, poking her finger at an area with multiple lines drawn to it.

"What are these?" Arslan asked, marveling at the sheer quantity of maps secreted in the room.

"Depends on the one you grab," Charlotte said, uneasy at the memories the collection brought up. "My…that is, Lauren loved cartography, and mapping the mystic leylines that went active after magic spread across the world. Sometimes I think she'd take runs in uncharted zones just to marvel at the lay of the land. Most of these are just grounder maps with her own notations, but this was one of the areas where the Earth's own nadir converged into a nexus point."

The Doll looked down at the map that had been spread out, his golden eyes widening as he read the name where the Earth's own hidden network of mystic veins merged.

"Arslan Tash" was the name of the location where they converged, about a hundred miles from the nearest town on the map.

"This…this cannot be coincidence," Arslan stated numbly.

"You think?" Charlotte asked sarcastically, fighting against the memories of Lauren the wall of maps conjured up. "I'd thought the Matriarchy put Godmother above the coast to conduct surveillance on the Ottomans after their massacre in Bulgaria. But this…this is what they're really here for."

Arslan traced the lines Lauren had carefully marked on the map in red and blue ink, the various tethers of mystic energy converging on a spot in the Syrian desert. His movements were slow and thoughtful, his eyes half-lidded. It was as if he had discovered evidence of a family generations-lost, a fascination Arslan couldn't help but indulge in.

"Do you know anything about this place?" Arslan asked, pale fingers idly tracing the map point.

"A bit," Charlotte said, rubbing the control ruby on her forehead. They were sitting ducks in the desert for anyone, and it was almost a physical itch to get airborne again to some measure of safety. "Arslan Tash was an ancient temple to Ishtar, the Mesopotamian goddess of love. It was discovered by some archaeologists a few years ago, although they were quickly driven off by the Ottomans. What it has to do with an advanced construct like you is anyone's guess. As far as I know, even the locals steer clear of the place nowadays; the people claim it's haunted by night demons and scorpion-tailed wolves. Lauren had talked about us heading out there in our downtime, doing a bit of exploration and discovery, seeing what we could dig up before…well, before all this shit. She figured the ancient peoples knew about the leylines, the convergence there, and they'd fallen into worship of it, and that when the villagers converted to Islam, they buried the place to seal the deal on such a sinful past. I don't know; that kind of thing was more her wheelhouse than mine. If it don't clank I find it hard to pay a lot of attention to it."

"There is more to it than that," Arslan said airily, as if he were talking from somewhere far away. "Much more. Beauty. Joy. Community."

His golden eyes narrowed.

"Pain."

"You know something about the ruins?" Charlotte asked suspiciously.

The Doll shook his head. "No. Yes. I…am not sure. It is as if I am trying to read a book whose writing has faded to nearly nothing. Every time I reach out, the thoughts flee like darkness from the light."

Charlotte rubbed her temples in frustration. "Well, that's not ominous at all. Still, once we leave the Levant area, I doubt we'll be back this way any time soon, especially if Godmother decides to hover over the ruins. This might be our only chance to figure out what you are, who crafted you, and maybe most importantly: why. I still want to believe they didn't create you for domination; but that's damn hard to do right now."

The captain held up a hand to forestall Arslan's objection.

"Yeah, yeah," Charlotte said. "You think you were

born, not built. But that glitch thought is neither here nor there. First thing's first. We need to get airborne again before they send an actual Liberty Ship for us. Even if we had the mystic juice to pull the same trick as we did on the drones, I doubt that it would work on an airship piloted by another tantric practitioner. The drones were an emergency measure they used, not their first choice. If there'd been a captain ready and willing to pursue us, you'd be getting dismantled right now and I'd be…well, hell, I don't know. Exiled, maybe? Worse, if Erin had her way about things, I'm sure."

Taking that as his cue, Arslan reached down and cupped his flaccid cock and balls. He gripped it and stroked a couple of times. But it gave no indication of interest. There was an embarrassed look on his perfect face.

"I, um. I might need some encouragement…"

Charlotte barked a short laugh. "What, us arguing about your origins while we contemplate the doom chasing us doesn't send your flag up the pole? I'm not exactly in the mood myself. But we need to fuck, and fast."

Arslan shook his head. "That proclamation is not helping."

"I've got a few tricks," the captain said with a shrug, trying to be teasing, pleasing. But although she admired the Doll's perfect form, the situation and the memories of Lauren were haunting her. And unlike when the automaton was in their Tash form, Arslan and Charlotte had a different feel, a different flow between them. The same spark they'd felt for each other was somehow missing, even though the captain found him exceedingly handsome. "Let's head for the battery hold."

As they descended back down into the *Harlot's Promise* Charlotte did her best to put her thoughts in a more erotic place. From the way that Arslan clutched the tattered remnants of the dress closed it was apparent he was having the same trouble getting in the mood. There was none of the coquettish charm that Tash had demonstrated, none of the constant flirting lacing every word. But it puzzled the aviatrix. Why bother constructing a weapon that had performance anxiety? The power of a gun was that you pulled the trigger and it killed. It took next to no training compared to a sword or axe, and your emotional state mattered not one whit to the bullet. A shovel was always ready to bite the dirt, and a Doll was always ready to fuck. That was the way of the world. Tools did not rely on mood to function.

But this one did.

Charlotte pulled her aetheric goggles back on, surreptitiously glancing back at the Doll. Any man following in the captain's wake should have had no choice but to be stimulated, especially given the promise of pleasure to come. But the Doll's aetheric lines were dull and unresponsive to the cling of Charlotte's black flight leathers to her shapely rear. Although she didn't have the bosom of Tash or Erin, her ass had always been a delicious temptation to all who saw it, male or female. Even other aviatrixes who were used to being saturated in sexual energies still couldn't avoid giving her curvy and pert cheeks a second look. That the Doll had felt them, tasted the fruit of her loins, should have only enhanced the desire to return to worship at the altar of her ass. Yet Arslan showed no interest in it, even as the captain made the effort to wiggle it a little as they descended.

The flows of magic in Arslan's mystic nadi system were different than Tash's in more ways than simply being switched from female to male. The vagaries of the soul were as dark and unknown as deep space, but as unchangeable as the rules of the universe. The discovery of what each regarded as pain and pleasure, of what the soul truly craved and was satiated by, was the subconscious goal of every sentient. The knowledge of another was only truly answered by that understanding. Wishing didn't change what a person was and what would make them happy.

Charlotte stopped suddenly as she finally understood what she was seeing in Arslan's aura, the truth of his soul. The Doll halted before he could run into her, shifting uncomfortably under her intense gaze.

"We're going to take a slight detour," Charlotte said after a moment's consideration.

"But our pursuers—" Arslan started to object.

"Can bloody well take a number," the captain said, interrupting him. "Follow."

Arslan ducked his head in acknowledgement as Charlotte led him to the quarterdeck, throwing open a trunk and rummaging through the gear within. Half-finished prototypes of different inventions were tossed aside, contraptions of copper, crystal, and leather that either didn't work or worked in ways the Frost wives hadn't intended. At the bottom of the trunk the captain found what she was looking for and pulled them out with a happy exclamation.

The old work gloves were made of brown deerskin, cracked with age and ill-kept, their surface rough and unforgiving. Charlotte had cut them apart and wove in a lining of libidium wiring intertwined with copper before sewing them back together, and the internal metal threading felt cold on her skin as she slid them on. They were bulkier and thicker than she was used to, and ill-fitting as well, but all of that had been design choices to prove their theory. The gloves had worked, after a fashion, but even the Frosts had given up on them being practical and consigned them to the dustbin as a result.

Arslan looked at her with puzzlement, his gold eyes taking in the ugly brutish gloves.

"Captain? I do not understand."

"I've been meaning to ask you, Arslan: what happened to 'mistress?'" Charlotte inquired with a knowing smile, grabbing hold of Arslan's hand and dragging him back toward the stairwell as she tucked the gloves into her belt. His reaction to her touch only confirmed the aviatrix's suspicions, as she felt as much as saw his cock stir a little.

"Apologies. Mistress," Arslan responded. The word stilted and forced.

"No. Stop that," Charlotte admonished him, pulling the Doll down the steps. "I was only bringing it to your attention. Call me what's comfortable for you. Tash regarded me as her mistress. I am something different to you, and it was my own idiocy in treating you like a normal Doll that led me astray in realizing that."

The banks of dark batteries greeted them as the captain wove their path between the wiring and various parts she'd pulled apart in her vain attempt to find more power where there was none. When they reached their destination, she gave a wry grin to the confused automaton in tow.

Before them was the tantric accumulator that Charlotte had pulled completely apart, its battery core as naked and vulnerable as a newborn. Copper wiring laced with libidium curled in thick stalks from the unseated faceplate back into the battery compartment like an alien root plant pulled from the soil, still clinging to its home desperately to find solace. The tantric engineer had modified the back half of the accumulator with a pair of metal rods that fed directly into the power system.

"What are those?" Arslan asked, his curiosity getting the better of his tendency to follow the captain's lead.

"Handholds," Charlotte said with a teasing smile. "Specifically, a direct connection to the power system to leach off active sexual energy during the act."

"Um," the Doll asked nervously. "Who is supposed to hold on to those?"

Charlotte shrugged. "Initially, me. In the hopes that we could find a male before the Legion caught up with us, I altered it so that I could hold on to those rods while, well, while another rod slammed into me. It would allow whoever was mounting me to go all-out, and I'd transfer the magic right into the flight aura."

"A clever design modification," Arslan said, nodding appreciatively before casting his eyes down. "But there is a problem, captain. I'm sorry, but I—"

"Don't really find me attractive," Charlotte finished for him, gently.

"Oh, no, not that at all," the Doll hurried to correct. "You are a beautiful woman, a vivacious aviatrix who could bring stone to attention. I remember Tash's desire, her lust, her appreciation and adoration of both your physical and intellectual capabilities. But for some reason I cannot fathom, I do not share those feelings. And I appear to lack the capability to summon that interest, no matter how much we both require me to."

Arslan's wide shoulders slumped at his admission. He'd been trying the entire time since his metamorphosis to alter his responses to Charlotte.

"It does not have any logical sense to it," he lamented bitterly.

"Oh, honey," Charlotte said, reaching up to his chiseled face. "It makes perfect sense, and if I hadn't kept thinking of you as Tash, or a normal Doll, I would have realized it sooner."

"Perhaps you can stimulate my chakra externally?" Arslan said, trying to sound hopeful but with a dread hidden within.

"I could," the captain agreed. "But I won't. For any other Doll, it wouldn't matter. They're not sentient, so they can neither consent nor deny, like any other mindless tool. A screwdriver has no opinion on how it is used. But you. You're different, and in more ways than just being self-aware. I could bring you to erection, I could force you to fuck me by using magic. But the energy produced would be tainted, corrupted by such vile practices. Nothing good ever comes of that. And even if the ship were able to use it, even if we were able to escape, it would be corrosive to both the systems of the *Harlot's Promise* as well as my own spirit. While you would not share in the responsibility of the crime, you'd be harmed by it as surely as a fist shattering that perfect jaw of yours."

Arslan shook his head, frustrated with himself. "When I was Tash, I remember craving you, desiring you beyond merely escape. I do not understand what has changed."

Charlotte sighed. "I know. I didn't either, not at first. So amazed was I that you possessed a mind and a soul, I neglected to look any deeper. That was my mistake. Not only do you have as much life within you as any organic sentient, but yours is also far more varied, and appears to shift in form spiritually as you do physically. To wit: what Tash and Arslan want and need are as different as the needs of a conjoined twin to its sibling. You each have your own mind and desire, your own soul. And, as such, your sexual preferences are different as well."

The captain gave a little self-deprecating laugh at her own presumptions and how it had cost them valuable time. The Doll was still confused, although Charlotte could see the truth trying to burst free. So, she shrugged and put it as simply as she could.

"Arslan. Sugar. You're gay."

Chapter 6

"I have protocols for being attracted to both sexes, but I do not see how that precludes—" Arslan started before Charlotte cut him off with a wave of her hand.

"There you go, falling into what I told you in error," the captain said. "So intent was I in debating with you whether you were alive or not I inadvertently manipulated your own assumptions. I'm not sure you *have* protocols, Arslan. And even if you do, they've been self-modified by that strange dual soul you possess."

Arslan slammed an ivory fist into the dark battery bank in frustration, making Charlotte jump a little.

"So, what you are telling me," he said, gritting his teeth, "is that although I have somehow transformed into the ideal solution to our problems, my mere sexual preference is what will cost us our lives?"

Charlotte took his face into her hands and forced the automaton to look at her. "No. You are what you are, same as anyone else. It isn't a choice; it is simply the truth. Denying it would be as moronic as refusing to believe that gravity works or fire burns. The problem of identity has dogged humanity since before history began. What we want to be and what we *are* can be two vastly different things. And I'm not about to let you start down the path of self-hatred for not living up to some imagined external expectation. You got me?"

Arslan wrinkled his lip in self-scorn and tried to wrench free. Charlotte held on and refused to let him look away from her.

"I said: you got me? Because…I got *you*."

Slowly Arslan began to relax, but Charlotte could still feel his impotent anger at the edge of his aura.

"Listen," she said, releasing the Doll's face. "I need you. Not a false version of whatever you are. You. Only when we deal with facts can we work our way through a problem. It's like my mama used to say: wish in one hand and spit in the other and see which gets full faster. You accept reality, how things are, and then you work from there to your goal. Everything else is just pissing into the wind."

Arslan grunted, his eyes downcast, but the captain could see his shoulders relax.

"Okay, great, we got the basics of 'be true to yourself' worked out," Charlotte said, sighing heavily. "Now, we figure out how to trick you into thinking I'm someone else."

The Doll looked up in surprise. "Sorry, did I misinterpret what you were just preaching to me? Corrupted energy, the truth of the soul, that sort of thing?"

"No, you got it right," Charlotte said with an embarrassed shrug. "But there's more to your soul than right here, right now. Sexuality is a four-dimensional axis of hetero, homo, spatial, and temporal. Who you are and what you prefer can change over time, although for most people it doesn't. So, too, can the environment you live, the community you experience, shift and manipulate your sexuality, although frequently in ways that people don't anticipate. Right now, you exist in a section of the sexual matrix where you desire female-aspected energy the least. On a simplified two-dimensional line of gay to not gay you are very gay. There's no changing that. But to save our lives, we must fool your soul, if however briefly."

The look of confused disbelief on the Doll's face matched Charlotte's own internal doubts about what she was planning. Although a few of the other tantric engineers had experimented with ways to alter desires via illusionary interface, it was mostly looked at as a dark perversion of the Art. Central to the Matriarchy's mystic doctrine was that the soul was what it was; there was no changing that or fooling it, and the further a practitioner drifted from the ephemeral truth the more likely their creations and magic would fail...or worse, succeed in a horribly destructive way. No aviatrix had ever tried to seduce a gay man with magic; it would have only produced a resentful corrosive energy, at best. Although a variety of men with alternate sexualities were often spirited away along with abused women to safe havens, they were at best viewed as noncombatants by the Matriarchy. Even those who volunteered themselves up as test subjects or to try and generate male energy with their partners were rejected out of hand by the Crone Council. The hurt inflicted for millennia by other men had made the Matriarchy loath to trust even those they had rescued from death and oppression, those that they shared common values and concerns with. It was just another example of infuriatingly self-destructive prejudices the aviatrixes had inherited from the kingdoms of man.

Charlotte had theorized that providing sensations akin to what they expected might offer a way to harvest male-aspected energy from volunteers without corrupting the magic, using a combination of stimulation and imagination to eke out some form of sexual compromise with willing subjects. The Crones had forbidden her from continuing the research, claiming it was because Charlotte was drifting too close to perverting the Art. The captain believed it was more that a new field of fantasy-fed sexual resources would threaten the Council's exclusive domination of the Matriarchy and Godmother. Regardless, she had bowed her head to their remonstrations and told them she gave up.

But she had lied to them.

"We're going to try a little experiment in illusion," Charlotte said. Patting her flight leathers and bustier down she found the protrusions she was looking for, pulling seemingly innocuous brass and tin pieces from her clothing. Every aviatrix had her own tricks and little devices they utilized in rescue and reconnaissance operations, and what she was putting together out of the disparate pieces was one of Charlotte's most reliable toys. Although it worked best under the cover of night, she'd once been able to orchestrate jail escape in broad daylight with a particularly dull guard.

Charlotte seated the thin metal choker's last piece before she fastened it around her throat.

"There," the aviatrix said, her voice much lower and hoarser, as if she'd just smoked a hundred cigars and chased it with a barrel of whiskey. "That's better."

Arslan widened his eyes in surprise.

"Your voice…that is a man's voice."

Charlotte grinned, pulling the heavy gloves from her belt. "Good. I was afraid you watching me put it on would lend to a cognitive dissonance that might make it hard to think that."

Arslan shook his head. "You misunderstand me, captain. When I say you have a man's voice, I do not simply mean that you have deepened your speech to a masculine timbre. I can feel it within my mind; the sentient protocols I have are responding to you as if you are male."

Charlotte pulled wire ends out of the lining of the gloves, connecting them to a small copper lead on her goggles. There was a brief flash of sensation doubling, feeling and seeing the same reality, and then her perception leveled off to a combination of impulses she could manipulate.

"Oi, guv'nur, don't choo be doubting me abilities," Charlotte said in a terrible cockney accent, flexing her fingers in the big, bulky gloves. "In other words, yes, I know. That's what I designed it to do. This little circlet has gotten me out of more scrapes than I care to count. The Vocalator Choker is a tool of subtlety, of liberation."

"Fascinating," Arslan said, reaching forward and brushing his fingers over the burnished circlet. "Is this a device commonly used by your kind?"

"Other aviatrixes?" Charlotte snorted. "Not really. Turns out serving aboard Liberty Ships and styling ourselves as swashbuckling heroines has the side effect of bloating the ego. Most tantric engineers put their own spin on our base inventions, or at least pretend to. It is the height of social faux paus to admit you're using someone else's tech."

Arslan shook his head. "That sounds highly irrational. I do not think even my Tash form would understand that thought process."

"Knowledge and ego are forever enemies," Charlotte agreed. "If you can't admit you don't know everything, then how can you learn anything? Regardless, how do you find yourself reacting to my vocal change?"

The Doll cocked his head, brow furrowed. "I am not quite sure. Multiple urges and reactions are fighting in a fashion I believe is unusual in any sentient."

Charlotte nodded, turning back to the battery casing she'd pulled apart earlier. The wrench she'd been using was in easy reach, and after a few moments of banging and struggling on the apparatus the captain scrounged out a set of gleaming silver rods from the guts of the device. With a couple of curses and a lot of grunting she managed to pull enough of the innards of the battery out to bolt the rods into an upright position.

"Those," Charlotte said, nodding at the twin silver rods, "are accumulator leads. Well, they were. Now... they're handles."

Arslan gripped one of the sturdy rods, impressed by how stable it felt in its impromptu bracket. An electric tingling sensation ran through the Doll's frame, eliciting a gasp. He felt his penis shift a little, as if a serpent had heard the pitter-pattering of mice in its lair.

"This has the potential to be exhilarating," he rumbled, his voice smooth like aged bourbon.

Charlotte ran a gloved finger over the other rod. "That's rather the point, sugar. After I confirmed we were bone dry on fuel, I jury-rigged this setup for me to grab hold of and feed energy directly into the system with a partner mounting me from behind. At first, I'd hoped we could find a male nearby and seduce him into the ship. But we're in the middle of nowhere, and then you suddenly grew a dick, and yet…your sexuality is incompatible with that plan. But I might have a solution. I'm not the one who's going to hold onto those handles, Arslan.

"You are."

The confused Doll let go of the rod he'd been enjoying. As soon as the contact was gone so too was any trace of mystically-stimulated desire.

"You wish me to masturbate?" Arslan asked. "With the assistance of the rods' tingling I should be able to achieve erection and subsequent orgasm regardless of current mood, although obviously I will need at least one hand free. Is it so easy to provide the fuel then?"

Charlotte sighed. "I wish. If that could generate the magic we need fast enough, I wouldn't have gotten these gloves, and would have left you to discover exactly why a machine was built with testicles."

Arslan barked a laugh and waggled his flaccid penis at her like an ineffective sword. "Do you think I ejaculate acid?"

"That'd be less dangerous," the captain replied, her expression sobering Arslan's mirth. "No, I think that just like your female form you likely excrete a tantric-laced venom designed to control your victim. We've developed prophylactics that could stop a bullet, so I was willing to chance having you in me when we both thought you'd be up for it. But I cannot be what you crave. So…we need to get creative."

The Doll raised a speculative hairless eyebrow.

Charlotte held up her gloved hand and waggled her fingers in time with her smirk, pulling it firm against her skin.

"Turn around and grab the handles."

Arslan was uncertain what she intended, but after a moment's hesitation did as he was told. Charlotte couldn't help but savor the way he obeyed, as well as the sculpted muscular buttocks that tensed with his worry. Tiny silver runes glistened just under the ivory skin, and the golden gears at his joints whirled noiselessly. But even as her eyes were drawn to Arslan's gears her attention was drawn back to the immaculate derriere in front of her. She wasn't surprised to find that the Doll had been built with an anus; many of the aviatrixes liked to dominate their sex toys with strap-on phallic creations. Like everything else, Arslan's erogenous zones were hyper-realistic, and it was easy to forget he wasn't a flesh and blood man.

"Captain…I am not sure I enjoy anal sex," the Doll said, looking back over his shoulder with consternation as he took a firm hold on the silver rods. "As you say, I find myself attracted to other males; however, that does not necessarily mean that— "

"Close your eyes and shut your mouth."

Charlotte's voice was a masculine growl, an avalanche of strength that made Arslan's knees tremble in response as soon as he shut his eyelids tight. Although absent the true melding of minds she'd experienced with Tash, through the libidium-laced gloves Charlotte was able to feel more of what Arslan felt. A hazy masculine form began to take shape in his mind, muscular with broad shoulders, features obscured by a light brighter than the sun. The Doll gave a little jump as Charlotte grabbed his ass with the bulky gloves while she channeled mystic energy through the libidium lining.

To Arslan's senses the hands smacking his ass and cupping his cheeks were not leather gloves, but rather, rough and mannish hands. The illusionary sensations were uncanny; the Doll could feel the little hairs on the back of the phantom fingers as they kneaded and squeezed his buttocks. Bereft of sight, it was easy for Arslan to react as if the touch was that of a man. He threw himself into the illusion, trying to ignore the worry that if he disbelieved it would shatter the dream. The Doll's mind reached out for the blinding light, embracing the figure forming within, using the loyalty to his captain to reinforce her illusion, drawing a man forth from the pulsing starburst.

As the light receded the figure's skin was revealed to be tanned russet, a reddish-brown earned through a lifetime of leading armies from the front lines. Thick black hair was tangled in whirls across his body, matching the long wavy beard that was immaculately kept, even during the longest of sieges, tended by tongs and curlers with tiers carefully laid upon each other. Eyes of sharp hazel were set into a craggy face that any mountain would be proud to possess. Well-coifed and perfumed hair fell in ringlets to the fantasy man's collarbone, a lifetime of immaculate care obvious in its and the beard's raven sheen. The muscles moving under the fur-like pelt were of no spoiled princeling, but a king, a conqueror, in both battle as well as beds. Piercings adorned his body in various places, but the most exotic of body modification was reserved for his penis.

The man's cock was of average length and thickness, but the phantom king had gone out of his way to enhance it both for his lover's pleasure as well as his own. Tiny pearls had been placed under the skin, ridging him in a fashion that would make any lover scream in joy. The naked figure shimmered as if through a heat haze as robes and armor began to materialize around him, but Arslan dispelled the clothes before they could finish. He wished to see his man full and proud, with nothing in the way.

"Oh, Kudurri," Arslan thrummed low, reaching out to the figure in his mind. "You are so sexy, my beloved Beast."

Charlotte managed to conceal her surprise as she stroked the Doll, moving her hands to his thighs, using the illusion magic to make Arslan feel as if calloused hands were running fingers along his legs. The aviatrix had hoped that the Doll possessed enough imagination to allow the trick to work. But she had not expected a phantom lover to spring into existence along with a strange name in Arslan's head. The Doll's cock was rigid, curving up slightly with head engorged and ready.

Charlotte moved carefully as she manipulated the tantric energy of her aura while she interacted with the Doll.

Although she was able to utilize her own flight leathers and magic to cloak her appearance to Arslan's senses, one wrong move might snap him out of the fantasy world, dooming them both. She suspected that once broken such a spell would be impossible to replicate, as the falsehood of it would be like a splinter in the eye.

"Yes," she rumbled, her voice dripping with the male intonations from the choker. A ripple ran through their interacting auras as Charlotte increased the feel of a being held by a bear of a man as she wrapped her arms around Arslan in a comforting embrace. "It is I, Kudurri. Did you miss me, my love?"

"More than any mortal can imagine," Arslan sighed, running his hands over Charlotte's arms. She tensed, but the magic held, and to his senses it seemed as if large furry arms had encased him.

Charlotte was in unknown territory now, dangerously balancing the line between lies and truth. The deeper she sank Arslan into the mystic illusion, the more it could hurt him if he lost his way and began to believe. It was possible that his mind would cling too tightly to the phantom lover, that it would reject reality as anathema after the dream was revealed. There was a part of Arslan that knew it wasn't real, that they were trying a desperate gambit, but at the same time there was a section of his soul yearning for a lover. An awfully specific lover.

The aviatrix paused as the image flickered briefly in her mind. No, not just any erotic figure had been called forth from the Doll's imagination. Charlotte realized from the mystic link that this wasn't some formless fantasy given life.

Arslan didn't want just any man. He wanted *this* one. The phantom lover wasn't a dream.

He was a memory.

The aviatrix faltered, and so too did the link. But even as the illusion blinked, Arslan's subconscious struck like a crocodile through the water, latching its jaws around the edges of the dream and clamping it together, stitching it firmly in place.

The Doll wasn't going to let it end that easily.

"Husband," Arslan growled enticingly, rubbing his backside into Charlotte. "You have been gone to the field for far too long. My long nights were made chilly without my furry beast holding me. Will you not demonstrate how much you have missed me?"

The lust coming off Arslan was almost palpable, and despite the circumstances Charlotte found herself becoming aroused. The aviatrix fought it off, centering herself with breathing techniques. If she wanted to keep from harming her newfound friend, she had to be careful with how they used the shared illusion. Arslan had to be the focus; were she to start cavorting in the fantasy there was too much of a danger of a utilitarian moral choice becoming a selfish one.

"And exactly how would you have me pray at your altar?" Charlotte said, her voice a smoldering fire as gloved hands reached around to the Doll's front.

Arslan gave a gasp when the hand wrapped around his rising cock. To his senses his husband had taken firm hold of his dick, the comforting weight and strength of the war-calloused hand beginning to stroke up and down. The Doll's sex was rigid with need, and his grip on the silver rods of the accumulator tightened as the speed of the stroking began to increase, timing the beat like a human heart. Arslan tensed his artificial muscles as he ground his hips in time to the beat, forcing the captain to stroke harder to keep rhythm.

"Oh, you know I like it when you tease," Arslan said to the bearded man in his dreams. Endless nights of pleasure in satin and silk rolled through his mind, a river of sensation whose currents matched the pumping of the gloved hand.

"Who said I was teasing?" the ghost replied, a fingertip running down to Arslan's ass. With a false shyness the finger explored around the Doll's anus, tracing the pucker as it slowly worked its way inside. "Perhaps tonight is the night."

"Every night is that night if you want, my beast," Arslan hissed, moving his ass back so that Kudurri's finger went in. The stroking on his cock matched the rhythm, and Arslan found himself fucking the gripping hand and the penetrating finger as he thrust back and forth.

Charlotte pumped harder on the Doll's cock as the automaton wriggled between her hands, his grip on the silver rods clenched. Amethyst sparks spilled from Arslan's body, bright and glaring to the captain's aetheric goggles. The pull to join Arslan in his fantasy was almost irresistible, and Charlotte found herself regretting she hadn't built a strap-on instead of gloves. Erotic energy charged the air with a purple haze, saturating the world.

In his mind Arslan felt his bearded lover stroking him, the bulge of his partner's cock as it pressed into the small of his back, the tiny pearls in its shaft promising good times to come. The smells of horse, leather, and blood from the king's latest conquests filled his nostrils, a forbidden spice that both excited and repulsed him at the same time. Their fights over it, over Kudurri's refusal of the Gilgamesh Protocol, of night arguments turned to passionate lovemaking, of—

"I'm coming!" Arslan roared as he thrust forward as far as the captain's grip would allow. "Yes, YES!"

Sticky translucent fluid shot out of Arslan's cock and onto the open battery as the captain pumped harder. The aetheric sparks the Doll was shedding became lightning bolts that arced from his illuminated skin, and the interior of the engine hold flashed like a thunderstorm over the mountains. The amethyst lightning heated the air, and the resultant boom as the bolts flashed nearly blew the captain's eardrums out. The sheer amount of power released was staggering, far in excess of what Charlotte expected.

Engulfed in the middle of the mystical maelstrom, the aviatrix held on by sheer strength of will, using the blazing control ruby on her forehead to channel the wild erotic energy into the batteries and subsystems of the aircraft. The dim crystal ship lights blazed hot and bright as power suffused the hull of the entire vessel, and the *Harlot's Promise* groaned in ecstasy as her flight aura sputtered back to life.

Charlotte held on for dear life as Arslan spasmed in time to his orgasm, shooting his venom across the battery where it lay glistening with an energy that transcended the physical plane. The aviatrix stroked in time, slowing and loosening her grip on his cock as it expended the last of its load.

Arslan was panting when he released the silver rods, their surface scorched black by the sheer amount of energy he'd just rammed into the system. Charlotte was sweating with their efforts as they both fell back together from the battery in a tired heap.

Lights played across the crystal-imbued surface of the battery, and the accumulators on its neighbors glowed as they pulled in excess power. Arslan's venomous ejaculate was slowly absorbed into the surface of the battery, leaving nary a trace in its passing as the fluid was converted entirely into energy.

Charlotte and Arslan chuckled in exhaustion from where the aviatrix held him on the floor.

"Are we fated to end up as such every few hours?" Arslan said, his voice a bit hoarse from the ecstatic screams.

"Apparently. Although as destinies go, I can think of worse," Charlotte giggled, although her attention was drifting as she accessed the control ruby to run a system check.

The stabilizing touch of the ship link sobered her, and for once she cursed how effective it was at clearing her mind. Charlotte's stomach felt as if she'd swallowed molten lead as she tackled the guilt that loomed over her. It was easy enough to ignore consequence in the heat of the moment and excitement of discovery, but there was no running from the implications of what had happened. The afterglow chilled with her tense, apologetic tone. "Look, Arslan, I'm sorry I didn't tell you exactly what I was going to do. By misdirecting your soul's perceptions, I managed to charlatan my way through it, but it required secrecy in execution. I figured that springing it on you might help to loosen your hold on reality and stay in the fantasy. We didn't have much choice, but that isn't much of an excuse either."

"I understand, Captain," Arslan said with a self-deprecating sigh. "There is no ill will for doing as you had to do. I am, after all, your servant, and serve as you please."

The aviatrix pushed him roughly off her, breaking the embrace as her anger rose volcanically.

"No!" Charlotte said, struggling to keep herself from shouting. "Stop that. Constructed or not, you have free will, a mind. Treating you as less than an equal debases both of us. That's why the research on enchantments is so restricted and reviled in the Art. Deceiving another's soul carries a consequence to one's own. Even with permission, there still might be unseen effects to be had. This isn't a schematic for the future; no more fucking between us. No matter how the mind justifies it, the soul rebels. And if we keep tempting Fate, she will be a mighty bitch when she comes calling for her due."

"Be at peace, my captain," Arslan said. "It was unfair and petty of me to intimate that I am your unwilling slave. I do not hold this event against you. We did, after all, agree that such an outcome was required for our continued survival. I wished to be misled, to be drawn into the illusion. In truth, it was stronger than I expected a dream would be though. I am grateful that you kept control during the fantasy, for I fear there was none to be had from me."

Charlotte shook her head. "There's a reason for its

strength: that was no illusion of the imagined. You were remembering a real person, a man who either does or has existed."

"Truly? Who was he then?"

"You don't remember?" the aviatrix asked, puzzled.

"At first I did. And then I did not. It was as if someone opened a door for a few moments, but then slammed it shut again," Arslan said, tapping his skull with his knuckles as if asking to be let in. "It is most infuriating to possess the knowledge you so achingly need with no ability to access it."

The captain got to her feet with a grunt, helping Arslan up after.

"You seem to like furry men, if that helps any," Charlotte said with a grin. "I'm guessing that little fetish has something to do with your entire lack of any body hair."

Arslan barked a laugh. "Well, yes, and Tash as well very much enjoyed tasting you through the wild shrubbery, as it were. I suppose I do find such a differentiation from me fascinating, as does my counterpart."

"There was a man you called out to in the illusion, a 'Kudurri.' Does the name mean anything to you? He was apparently your husband and possessed some…skill at the erotic arts."

The Doll shook his head. "No, I am sorry. The shadows have returned to under the ice, and I am left with more questions than answers at their passing. Either way, it had the intended effect it seems. Your ship is operational."

"She's a tough old bird," Charlotte said affectionately, patting the interior bulkhead. "The seaward rudder is probably irrecoverable from us belly-flopping on it, but other than that we came through that emergency landing fairly intact. I'll take a closer look later, after we've made it to our destination and figured out how to hide ourselves."

"Destination?" Arslan asked. "I apologize, but my mind is still jumbled. Did we actually decide on where we are fleeing to?"

Charlotte gestured for him to follow as she headed for the stairwell. There were a lot of systems that were automatic, but she still needed to get topside to get a clear view of the horizon. She pointed vaguely east, the direction of the ruins they'd located on the map.

"Where else? We go where your name points us: Arslan Tash.

"Let's find out what in Lilith's name is really going on."

Chapter 7

There was a chill to the air as Charlotte emerged on the top deck. Night had crept up and blanketed the desert while they'd been refilling the batteries. Bereft of any real vegetation save for a few scraggly trees and tough bushes, the sand and rocks were quickly losing the heat of the day. With no moon in the sky, the stars blanketed the world above, a glittering tapestry of mystery and wonderment. With nothing to break up the view from horizon to horizon the sheer magnitude of the glittering sky was enough to humble even the most arrogant.

Arslan had peeled off at the quarterdeck, but he wasn't the captain's primary concern now. Through the control ruby she checked the power reserves and was pleasantly surprised. One battery brimming with masculine-aspected energy, and two others near it had caught the spillover from the excess. It wasn't a fully charged battery bank by any means, but it was more than enough to flee before the oncoming storm.

Dreading what she was going to find, Charlotte scanned the horizon with her aetheric goggles. Expecting the worst, she was again happily proven wrong as she saw no mystic trails from any pursuing ships. Yet. She wasn't quite sure why the entire fleet hadn't been mobilized to track down the advanced Doll she'd helped escape, but she wasn't going to look a gift horse in the mouth. Although there was no certain way of tracking other Liberty Ships when they weren't actively employing their flight aura, Erin and the Matriarchy were likely organizing a strike team to bring the *Harlot's Promise* down.

Given the Doll's mind control capabilities they wouldn't expect Charlotte to still have her free will, and that gave her an advantage. Erin was a straightforward kind of thinker; Occam's razor would be her mantra if she deigned to ever read anything written by a man. The thought that it'd be easy enough to hand over the Doll and claim innocence wormed its way into her worries, and Charlotte rejected it with disgust. That wasn't who she was. And it never would be.

Now that the *Harlot's Promise* was hovering above the ground, Charlotte could examine the damaged seaward sail through the control gem, noting how it had been completely crushed by the landing. The material it was constructed of contained no trace of libidium or other secret magics, so she sent the command to release the clamps on the damaged mast and sail. The ship bobbed up for a moment as the wreckage jettisoned with a pained screech. Although she wouldn't be quite as maneuverable without the seaward fin, the *Harlot's Promise* was still airworthy.

Charlotte opened her eyes, maintaining her link as she strode to the foredeck, boots heavy on the planks. There was something electric in the air beyond the mystic aura surrounding the ship, a feeling of a new beginning, of old damaged parts of her life falling away like the broken sail. The bittersweet tang of loss and a sublime beauty drew her forward. Charlotte couldn't quite explain it, but it felt as if the magic itself wanted her to follow this course. Had she been as religiously certain as her sisters, Charlotte would have said Lilith was guiding her.

"Well, who am I to deny the First Sinner," Charlotte murmured to the night air. No divine inspiration shone down on her, no angelic choir or demonic band rose to give their stamp of approval. But the darkness was welcoming and safe, and the stars sparkling in the firmament above felt like the universe watched with gentle approval.

The course to the Arslan Tash ruins was easy enough to plot, although the height stumped Charlotte for a moment. If she skimmed the ground, it would lessen the chances of detection by any pursuers. But without the seaward sail there was a real possibility of not being able to bank fast enough to avoid obstacles. And although the Ottoman Empire was backward in many ways, they still possessed firearms. Altitude was really the only protection most Liberty Ships had or needed.

Charlotte's back itched like a rifle was being sighted on it as she commanded the *Harlot's Promise* to ascend. A quick check behind revealed no pursuers, and the mystic pulses from the ground had zero trace of humanity to them. Given their limited stores of power, Charlotte chose a cruising speed that would have them arrive at the ruins in a couple of hours while using the least amount of energy. But the moment she detected another Liberty Ship fuel efficiency would become the least of her concerns and she'd channel everything into the engine pontoons. They'd been incredibly lucky so far, and that concerned Charlotte.

She didn't like relying on fortune; too many Liberty Ship captains had made that mistake and paid the price for it. Charlotte knew she was missing some vital piece of information that would change her perception. She was keenly aware of the absence, the void that affected what was going on as surely as a star affected a planet's orbit. The ignorance had its own gravity, and it was frustrating to not be able to see it. But there was nothing to be done except proceed with her plans and hope that she could deal with what popped up.

The next hour passed uneventfully. Charlotte spent the entire time staring back at the vanishing mountain range they'd flown over. Even stretching the ship's sensing apparatus to its limits, she couldn't detect any activity back that way. But there were a variety of tricks a canny aviatrix could utilize to hide their vessel's path, most of which were unavailable to the damaged *Harlot's Promise*. The lack of evidence of pursuit only made Charlotte more paranoid that she was missing something. That vital void nagged at her, forced second-guessing into her decisions.

"Oh, my. The night sky is uniquely beautiful, is it not?"

Tash's voice made the antsy captain nearly leap off the deck in surprise, yanking her aetheric goggles off to confront the real world. Although the Doll was front and center of her worries, Charlotte had shuffled the actual automaton to the periphery of her worry. The feminine tones told her that Arslan had shifted back to his female form before the aviatrix had even turned around, but she was still startled by what Tash was wearing.

The Doll had not only morphed back into her female form, but she had also been at the clothes rack on the quarterdeck again. But this time all attempt at dressing down to blend in had abandoned. Tash had apparently drawn the same conclusion as Charlotte: there was never any way she could truly hide, so why try?

Instead of a drab peasant dress the Doll had instead chosen a flowing off-white dress with yellow floral print complete with ruffles around its floor-length skirt. Tash's shoulders were bare, somehow appearing more vulnerable and sexier than when she'd been fully nude. The swell of her breasts was enhanced by a honey-colored bodice that allowed the small, ruffled straps to hang loose at her upper arms, drawing more attention to her flawless ivory shoulders. The Doll's skin was a pearlescent beauty that no linen could ever match, and Tash had used to her advantage. Delicate fingerless gloves and a cute little bonnet were the same shade of yellow as her bodice, completing the look.

It was as if a goddess of summer had descended to grace the mortals with her presence.

Tash twirled under the captain's admiring gaze, revealing shoes that matched the hat and bodice, as well as white stockings that tempted lovers to search out how far up they went. "So...what do you think? I found this lovely bonnet, and the dress just went perfectly with it."

Charlotte gave an appreciative nod. "Gorgeous as always. I see we're no longer trying to wear potato sacks to disguise ourselves?"

Tash giggled, making a show of covering her mouth with her gloved hand like a proper lady. "I realized that the more I tried to hide what I was, the more obvious I became. If I am to be stared at, then I shall give them something to see."

"That's actually a good point," Charlotte said. "You might occasionally blend, to those not used to a delicate lady. Humans are fond of names and concepts they can easily grasp; they need a concept they can hang their hat on. Better a noble whose skin has never seen the sun than wondering who kidnapped a princess and made her a pauper, eh?"

"Just so," Tash nodded. "And since Arslan was fatigued from assisting you, he relinquished our form to me for the time being. So, I decided to give you something pleasant to look at. Besides…I missed you."

The remark caught Charlotte off-guard.

"I thought you and Arslan shared memories?" the captain asked.

Tash stroked her own cheek with a contemplative look. "Yes, but only memories after the fact. Current thought patterns and choices are left to the individual in control. The other slumbers as the active takes the reins. But you can be assured, mistress, that my dreams are only of you."

Charlotte felt the heat from her blush and hurried past the unexpected adoration. "Well at least one of you desire me. Poor Arslan, he wanted so hard to be what I needed. The magical handjob was as close as he could get."

The Doll tittered. "Indeed, he does miss his Kudurri,

whoever that is. Right now I can feel his dreams of the man. I am unsure as to when we encountered his lover, or for how long, but the feelings are quite real. Arslan and I both eagerly wait for the fantasy to call us by name, to free the shadows from the ice."

"You think some sort of pet name will crack the surface to the rest of your memories? I mean, I suppose that's one way in, but it doesn't seem strong enough to break through whatever block is on your mind," Charlotte replied absent-mindedly, her attention focusing back on where their pursuers should be but weren't. She itched to put the goggles back on and resume sentry, but it felt rude to tell the Doll to bugger off so she could return to work.

Tash looked confused. "No, mistress. I think the revelation of my real name would be a key factor in reclaiming my identity."

It took a moment for what she'd said to penetrate Charlotte's growing paranoia.

"Wait, what?" the captain said, finally processing the Doll's meaning. "You were named after the ruins we're flying to, right?"

"You appear to be confused, mistress," Tash said, gentle as a mother teaching a child. "The appellation 'Arslan Tash' was not given to me. I chose it."

Charlotte shook her head in confusion. "Seriously? Like I said—"

"Truly, must we again debate my origins?" the Doll interrupted, a hint of irritation creeping into her voice. She held up a hand to forestall Charlotte's reply. "Regardless, mistress, in the realm of objective truth I tell you this: I was named by myself."

"I am so lost," Charlotte said, rubbing her temple. "Why would you choose so arcane and obscure a name, and how the holy hells did you even know of those ruins? I barely remembered it from an old map Lauren was messing with, and she only knew of it due to months of dusty research."

Shrugging her lovely bare shoulders, Tash replied, "They were the first words I knew after awakening, and they seemed particularly important for some reason. The choice to refer to myself as such was a bulwark against further memory loss."

Charlotte ran a hand over her face. "So, let me get this straight: the only person who knows your name is me?"

"More a nom de guerre than my true name, but yes."

"No one else called you that? Not Erin, not Godmother, no one?"

Tash looked confused, and a hint of ice crept into her voice. "I believe I have been quite clear on that point, Captain. Is there something wrong with naming myself?"

An incredulous laugh escaped from Charlotte. "No, but I wish you'd have told me that a couple of hours ago. It would have saved a lot of worry and stress on me."

"How do you mean, mistress?"

Charlotte gestured back at the mountains on the horizon, outlined by their obstruction of the night stars. "Here I've been sweating an enemy descending on us at any moment, thinking they knew precisely what our destination was, while all the time they're clueless as to where we're headed! For the love of Lilith...does anyone on Godmother even know about Arslan Tash in the first place?"

"As far as I am aware?" the Doll answered. "No."

Charlotte threw her arms to the sky and hollered a relieved shout. She rushed to Tash's side and grabbed the automaton's hands, pulling her close.

"We're free, sugar!" Charlotte shouted in joy.

"Mistress," Tash tried to interject as the aviatrix spun her around breathlessly. "Charlotte. Captain Frost!"

The Doll's alarmed tone brought Charlotte up short. "Tash? What's wrong?"

Tash looked worried. "I do not believe you have cause to celebrate. It occurs to me that your sisterhood's presence in this region is too coincidental, even if I did name myself. And whether your supposition of my origin or my own are correct, the fact remains that such an obscure name and location is tied directly to me. If that is the case, whether named by others as such or not, there is every reason to believe that the Matriarchy knows of the ruins. And although it may not occur to them immediately..."

The implication hung in the air like an icy stalactite, a spear of terror waiting to fall and pierce their hearts. Neither of them spoke, but both understood the simple and brutal reality. Even if Lauren didn't think to look for them at Arslan Tash, the chances were high that others knew of the ruins. Just because they didn't have the entire Legion breathing down their necks yet didn't mean they were free and clear. It was only a matter of time until someone came hunting this direction.

Their jubilant mood was dampened by the realization;

they crossed the dark ribbon of the Euphrates in silence as they continued sailing east through the sky. The lights of a village near the shore were dim compared to the majesty of the stars above, but the light of humanity was a warm reminder of home and hearth to Charlotte. No matter the source, when people gathered around fire it felt as if they shared a bond beyond the heat, the most primal expression of pack and tribe that stirred within every person's heart.

As they passed over the village a startled shout rang out, and a rifle fired right after. But under the blanket of the moonless night the *Harlot's Promise* flew on unharmed, the bullet missing by a country mile. Charlotte, her hands extended to help focus as she directed the ship via her control ruby, laughed at the shot, drawing an odd look from Tash.

"That's actually rather comforting," Charlotte explained, pulling her mind out of the link. "It makes things seem almost normal to have a grounder take a potshot at us."

"They may not all be as unaware and inaccurate as that particular admirer," Tash cautioned.

Charlotte chuckled. "They usually aren't. Don't worry, the hull of any airship is reinforced enough to shrug off anything smaller than a cannon. Plenty of marksmen have celebrated hits on us without doing anything other than wasting lead, time, and paint."

"You are not invulnerable, mistress," Tash chided. Her tone had gotten slightly sharper, and Charlotte noticed the Doll was on edge.

"I'm well aware of my own mortality, Tash," she said,

moving behind the Doll so she could hug her in a comforting embrace. Charlotte pulled Tash close and snuggled in against the back of the taller Doll, propping her cheek up on Tash's shoulder. The automaton gratefully held onto the captain's arms encircling her, leaning her own head down to gently press against Charlotte's.

"What's really wrong, Tash?" the aviatrix asked. The way they held each other was more familiar, more intimate, than any sex.

"It feels dangerous, life-threatening, world-ending," the Doll said with a shiver.

Charlotte kissed Tash's bare shoulder, nuzzling in. "Don't worry about it, Tash. If they haven't started this direction yet we can keep ahead of them, even with our quick stopover at the ruins."

Tash became very still. "No, mistress, you misunderstand. I do not fear what is behind us.

"I fear what lays before us."

The Doll pointed out across the bow into the darkness ahead. Chills ran up Charlotte's spine, and she pulled away from their embrace to raise her goggles again. She didn't expect to see much. The world was normally a ghostly outline to aetheric sight, and it took time and experience to ignore the outlines of the ship's hull and other obstructions to properly navigate. Low levels of ambient mystic energy ran through the world everywhere, and although leylines were heavy in the area they should have been little more than a thicker outline amid a world of hollow images. The captain had already begun slowing the ship down to make sure she didn't overshoot the ruins.

She needn't have bothered.

Darkness melted away under the scrutiny of the alchemically-treated lenses, revealing far more magic in the area than Charlotte expected. Light broke through the ground in jagged lines, a bright spiderweb of cracks that led directly to the Arslan Tash ruins ahead. It was as if the old temple had shattered the world and fractures of chaos were shining through the edges.

The ruins themselves wouldn't have been much to see without the goggles. Lauren hadn't been sure which god the temple had been dedicated to, but religious zealots had buried it as a sign of their faith when they'd converted millennia ago. The British archaeologists who'd uncovered it had only been able to excavate the entrance, a wide arch with twin black stone lions guarding the entrance. But continued skirmishes with the locals had driven them off, and the site had been abandoned for a long time. Fear and superstition had protected the temple far better than any guard could. To the unaided eye, the ruins were little more than a hole in the hillside with a couple of decrepit statues. With the aetheric goggles though, the truth was revealed.

A massive complex of tunnels and buildings spread under the earth to the horizon, the full scope and magnitude revealed by the echoes of light that ran through the preternaturally charged walls of the hidden temple.

"What in the world is this place?" Charlotte breathed, wonderment filling her mind. "Even Godmother does not glow as this place does, and she has libidium walls. How have we never discovered such a rich site of aetheric energy before?"

Tash laid a hand on the aviatrix's arm, pulling Charlotte out of her reverie.

"Mistress," the Doll said. "What makes you think the Matriarchy is ignorant of this place?"

Charlotte shook her head. "No, that can't be. I've never even heard of Arslan Tash before. There'd have been rumors, legends, something."

"Anonymity is a far better guardian of secrets than any wall," Tash responded.

"No, it doesn't make sense," Charlotte continued to object. "Do you know how many people would have to keep their mouths shut to cover this up? Are you seriously trying to tell me that…Tash…what are you doing?"

The Doll had walked forward until she was at the edge of the bow of the ship, spreading her arms as if praying to the stars above, a figurehead of Victorian beauty.

"Proving a supposition and settling the argument, my hard-headed mistress," Tash said over her shoulder, her attention focused on the ruins.

Thunder cracked the air without any lightning. It took the captain a moment to realize the sound was not coming from the clouds.

It was coming from the ground.

The desert in front of the ruins split asunder, a crack forming that separated into two halves of moving earth as trees and rocks tumbled down into the dazzling light it revealed. Tash was chanting something incomprehensible, and through the goggles Charlotte saw subtle tendrils of magic stretching out from the Doll to the ground below. Where there had once been solid unassuming ground, there was now an opening massive enough to fly half a dozen airships into.

The brilliant aetheric light spewing from the revealed entrance made the aviatrix tear off her goggles before she was blinded by it. Without her mystic sight the entrance that had been revealed was naught but a dark abyss yawning wide in the middle of the scrub desert, larger and more sinister than the gates of Hell itself.

"How...Tash, how did you do that?" Charlotte asked numbly.

The Doll lowered her arms, her expression inscrutable.

"I do not know, mistress. But I am eager to discover the answer."

Tash turned to Charlotte, vulnerability and fear breaking down her calm facade.

"Mistress. I must know my origins, the meaning behind all of this. I will go on without you if forced to...but I would prefer to have you at my side. I will employ no tricks, no venom, no mental alteration to convince you to accompany me. I merely beg, with all my heart: help me face the truth. Please."

Charlotte reached up to the Doll's cheek, her fingers lightly brushing the ivory skin. Magic flowed through Tash, centered on her, and for the first time the aviatrix finally admitted to herself that she was feeling something other than admiration for the impossible automaton. Something that had been damaged by the careless actions of her ex-wife, something she'd feared they had stolen from her. It was only a spark, a beginning, but Charlotte knew better than anyone else what it could develop into.

Love.

"I won't abandon you, Tash," the captain said, emotion suffusing her words. "We've come this far together. I will stand by your side as we descend into the darkest depths."

Tash closed her eyes, nuzzling against her captain's hand.

"Thank you, mistress," she whispered. "I do not wish to be alone."

A lump formed in Charlotte's throat, her own loss and pain gaping as wide as the chasm below them.

"No one does, sugar. And no one should have to be."

Captain and Doll pulled each other into a kiss of promise as they descended from the skies to their destiny.

END BOOK 1

About the Author

Award-winning author Timothy Black was born in the Deep South where he hit the road at an early age and quickly learned it could hit back. Driven by an insatiable curiosity, he studied Geology, Astronomy, and the Occult, ending up with a degree in Philosophy that twists through his writing. After traveling the world to find his great loves he settled down in the Pacific Northwest, determined to craft stories that defy confinement to any single genre. A serial killer of coffee and whiskey sours, he stays one step ahead of retribution with a rebellious cackle and knowing wink.

Facebook: facebook.com/timothyblack.author/
Twitter: @Tim_RFP

Also by Timothy Black
Published by Dreamsphere Books

Gearteeth
Timothy Black

On the brink of humanity's extinction, Nikola Tesla and a mysterious order of scientists known as the Tellurians revealed a bold plan to save a world ravaged by a disease that turned sane men into ravenous werewolves: the uninfected would abandon the Earth's surface by rising up in floating salvation cities, iron and steel metropolises that carried tens of thousands of refugees above the savage apocalypse.

Twenty years later, only one salvation city remains aloft, while the beasts still rule the world below. Time has taken its toll on the miraculous machinery of the city, and soon the last of the survivors will plummet to their doom. But when Elijah Kelly, a brakeman aboard the largest of the city's Thunder Trains, is infected by the werewolf virus, he discovers a secret world of lies and horrific experiments that hide the disturbing truth about the Tellurians.

When the beast in his blood surges forth, Elijah must choose between the lives of those he loves, and the city that is humanity's last hope of survival.

Available in ebook and paperback!

More from Deep Desires Press

The Frozen Prince
Minna Louche
He is her captor, cursed by ice magic and hiding a deep secret, yet Genevieve can't help the feeling of desire growing in her heart as she is drawn into the mystery of the frozen prince.

Desire and Witchery
Christopher Stires
I am witch's animal companion, in the legendary appearance of a male black cat. I vow to protect Milady in all ways possible, alas, I may not be able to shield her from her own desires when the Captain comes into our lives.

One Task
Geneva Gordon
Tig is a woman whose celebrity status has propelled her career from special operative to a pending career in film. But none of her skills, experience, or determination have prepared her for the dangerous journey ahead, as she is transported to the distant past, to the strange land of Moregane, where danger and love await her in one task that will forever change her.